CW01091632

1

SHARDS

A novella by Cynthia Rumbidzai Marangwanda

2nd edition published in Great Britain in 2023 by:

Carnelian Heart Publishing Ltd
Suite A
82 James Carter Road
Mildenhall
Suffolk
IP28 7DE
UK

www.carnelianheartpublishing.co.uk

Copyright ©Cynthia Rumbidzai Marangwanda 2023

Paperback ISBN: 978-1-914287-40-4

E-book ISBN: 978-1-914287-41-1

1st published in Zimbabwe in 2014 by LAN Readers

A CIP catalogue record for this book is available from the
British Library.

This novella is a work of fiction. The names, characters and
incidents portrayed in it are the work of the author's
imagination. Any resemblance to actual persons, living or
dead, is purely coincidental.

All rights reserved. No part of this publication may be
reproduced, stored in a retrieval system or transmitted in any
form or by any means, electronic, mechanical, photocopying,
recording or otherwise without prior written permission from
the publisher.

Editors:
Lazarus Panashe Nyagwambo &
Samantha Rumbidzai Vazhure

Cover design & Layout:
Rebeca Covers

Typeset by Carnelian Heart Publishing Ltd
Layout and formatting by DanTs Media

To my father and mother, for the unconditional love.

To my son, husband, sister and brother, for the unwavering support and encouragement.

It's half-past failure and I'm still in bed. The date is twenty-three, same as my age. My wrists have seen better days, battle-scarred and war-wounded as they are. My arms are riddled with bullets. They stopped bleeding when I stopped feeling at the age of seventeen. That is when a father figure grabbed me by the throat and threatened the innocence out of me. His wife was not there to witness it; she was away weeping hot pious tears on her knees in a house of worship or wailing theatrically on all fours at a fellow churchgoer's funeral. Or maybe she was too busy trying to cope with the delights of motherhood. God bless wombs and all the poison they bring forth. My sister was away at school painting her fresh-faced adolescence all over a paedophilic education system.

I raise my head slightly to catch a glimpse of the familiar cream-coloured wall I have confronted for a period longer than time. The same damn wall! I hum an obscure tune as I coerce my legs to leave the refuge of my blankets. Their stiffness is a silent protest. I notice my new laptop in the corner of the room. It looks so modern and functional I wish to kick it. My other sibling kicked me once. He kicked me like a township soccer ball. I didn't bounce. I fell down on my parents' marble tiled kitchen floor and screamed that I was going to end my life. I didn't. Not yet at least. This incident with my other sibling happened about the same time a father figure cornered me by the throat.

My bookshelf is any space not occupied by the overused bed and lengthy closet in my room. My feet sink into a river of books floating comfortably on the grass-coloured carpet. None of them is a Bible. I find popular fiction unpleasant. I eye my bed warily. The logical thing to do would be to spread it, but my laziness is wielding its persuasive influence again. My books watch me numbly. If any of my aunts from my mother's side were here, they would tell me it's unwomanly not to spread your bed and tidy your room. They would warn me that if I harbour any hope of ever salvaging a husband for my unwed self, then I should act more proper, be more groomed. After little thought I decide to leave my bed in peace, undisturbed. It needs to rest. I grab a towel from the turmoil that is my closet shelf and drag my limbs to the shower. The bathroom looks so clean and sanitised I have no choice but to promptly vomit on its sparkling floor. I purposely avoid the toilet chamber. My intention is to mar. I notice a piece of the national flag in my vomit. I wonder if I will also pass out a section of my citizenship the next time I move my bowels.

The shower looms like a gas chamber. I turn the faucet and allow the water to sedate me. I don't know how long I stand there, not touching the soap or the towel. Cinematic scenes play on the screen of my mind. Snapshots of memory click on and off. The water hums a warm chorus. My skin wrinkles, peels off and comes to rest in a crumpled heap at my feet. The water shrieks a cold ballad. My heart beats a hallucinatory percussion. The water loses its voice and croaks hoarsely. Dry air assaults me. I bend down and gather up my dejected skin. When I put it back on I discover it still fits. I don't find this particularly pleasing. I trudge back to my room and halt in front of my full-length mirror. I stare trance-like at my nakedness. I look decidedly unfuckable. I play Brenda Fassie as I rummage through my piles and piles of clothes. It's not a weekend and I don't feel special, but my meagre hips still sway to her scandalous voice. I can't seem to find any garment worth wearing. I eventually settle on something inexplicable before heading to the cavernous kitchen downstairs to mute my noisy stomach.

I find our housekeeper bent over the stove. Because she is a relative, she is not obliged to wear a maid uniform, and besides, this isn't Rhodesia. The intensity with which she is stirring the pot is eerie. I want to peer and check if she is not preparing human meat for dinner. She casts me a slanted glance, the type a cat would throw a mouse asking for directions, and I'm compelled to pass a polite greeting. She answers in a strained, high-pitched voice, and I notice for the umpteenth time how her mouth puckers at the corners when she speaks. It's not very attractive. She once accused me of witchcraft. I was so infuriated I went and spent an entire night sticking safety pins into a voodoo doll hastily made in her likeness.

I make toast, baked beans, sausage and eggs for myself, along with tea. How I still afford to look so emaciated when I eat this much confounds me. The food tastes inedible and the tea is equivalent to sewer water. I think of all the harrowing footage of starving Africans I see on CNN and BBC and guilt makes me finish my meal.

When I'm done, I wash my plates and tell the housekeeper I'm going out. She throws me an angular look, the type a crocodile would cast a fisherman standing by the river, and nods. I walk outside and pass our gardener mutilating the hedge. I wait as the electric gate slides open before stepping out to confront a waiting wilderness.

My legs feel stilted as I make the short walk to the bus-stop and wait for a *kombi*, a minibus taxi. When it arrives, I get in and sit by the window. I register virtually nothing as the vehicle moves towards the city centre. There is nothing much to notice anyway, just a lot of brownness. The only noteworthy occurrence happens halfway to town when an elderly white man boards the *kombi*. All of us cannot help but stare. There is something slightly askew about his presence in the vehicle, something invasive, like a colonial settler invasion or a farm invasion, perhaps. The rest of the journey is uneventful.

The *kombi* eventually stops at a place that is supposed to be a bus rank but is in fact chaos-in-motion. I ask the grumpy conductor for my change but he is uncooperative. I decide not to pursue the issue. The state of his shoes informs me he probably needs the coins more than I do. I get out and am immediately assailed by the aroma coming from the nearby public toilet. I walk past people buying vegetables from the makeshift market stalls adjacent to the toilet. A bleach-skinned woman wearing a platinum blonde weave bumps into me and neither of us bothers to apologise. A man with a predatory face makes a suggestive comment in my general direction as I pass. Two police officers stand on a street corner holding their truncheons restlessly. And the blue glass of a newly-constructed skyscraper winks at the sun.

I hear a familiar sound, a message on my cell phone. It reads, 'Are you coming?' I type, 'Yes just a few minutes away' and press send. In a short while, my tennis shoes turn into a dusty yard housing a melancholy block of flats, located on the outskirts of the CBD. An assortment of under-dressed females stand near the entrance, waiting for business to come calling. They eye me conspiratorially. I pretend they are not there and quicken my pace. My tennis shoes walk up some stairs and stop in front of door number 74. I assault the door with my knuckles and wait. I hear the shuffling of feet and incoherent mumbling. The door flies open and a riot of dreadlocks dressed in a vest and frayed jeans wave me in. I walk into a pigsty of a bedsit reeking of an all too familiar smell. My nose wrinkles.

"Your place stinks," I inform the dreadlocks leaning against a wall, observing me.

"So? My place is perpetually putrid," the dreadlocks point out, in a voice like opaque beer.

"You could at least open the windows," I chide and proceed to do just that. "So who was it last night?" I ask disinterestedly.

"Who was what?" The dreadlocks feign ignorance.

"Who.did.you.screw.last.night?" I say it as if pronouncing a spelling.

A thoughtful pause follows. I take the opportunity to deposit my thinness on the weathered mattress sleeping on the floor.

The dreadlocks pull deeply on a just lit cigarette and ask, rather vaguely, "Why do you care?"

"I care because your place stinks of sex and I'm curious," I retort.

"Veronique," the dreadlocks say simply. I digest the name for a moment.

"The French girl? But she didn't seem like she fancied you much."

"It's amazing how revolutionary a bit of wine can be," the dreadlocks announce wryly.

"Hmm…well as long as you enjoyed yourself."

"Hardly. It was a lot of hair, French cuss words, fingernails and not enough sensation. Nothing worth writing a poem about," the dreadlocks inform me. I blink and say nothing. A restless hand runs through some dreadlocks.

"I'm hungry, we should get something to eat," a vest and jeans tell me.

"Did your one night stand leave you any money?" I ask.

"Yes, a fairly adequate amount. Did your father give you your month's allowance?" The dreadlocks watch me closely.

"Yes he did," I answer tonelessly.

"That's good, that's real good. Don't you have lectures today? Shouldn't you be at campus?" a dreadlocked voice enquires.

"Learning in lecture halls leads to lobotomies. Fuck varsity," I say coolly. The dreadlocks grin wickedly.

"Alright, little girl."

I notice a pair of unfinished paintings disintegrating next to an Olivetti typewriter.

"What do you intend to do with those?" I gesture in their direction.

"Abandon them."

"Hmm. I think those sex workers by your gate think I'm your girlfriend," I declare indignantly.

"Of course they do. They fancy themselves specialists on the mating games between boys and girls."

A meaning-laden pause ensues. We both seem to be waiting for him to decisively address the question mark floating conspicuously around the room. When he doesn't, I simply shrug my shoulders. A delicious burst of sunlight erupts inside the room and the lizard in me approves. I slip out of my insecurities and deposit them next to a congregation of empty wine bottles. I stretch my nakedness across the length of the mattress and welcome the smell of cigarette smoke scenting my skin.

I remember how the dreadlocks and I met. We used to frequent the same places without our paths ever quite intersecting. In those days I was being courted by a pan-Africanist filmmaker type who referenced Kwame Nkrumah and Steve Biko every time he unsealed his lips, which was often. Needless to say, I was spectacularly bored. I was then enrolled at a different tertiary institution from the one I am currently attending. I hardly attended lectures there either, and I inevitably dropped out. There was far too much living to do and I found – and still find – formal education to be a sort of suffocating death-by-pedagogy, so I chose to avoid this glaring ritual of mortality with as much might as I could muster.

In those days, I wore only floor-sweeping African-print dresses and earth-coloured sandals. All my jewellery was wooden or beaded, and I delighted in horrifying my mother by staunchly refusing to comb my unruly natural hair – a habit I never gave up. When I walked down the streets, I would get shouts of "Empress!" and "Jah sistren!" from men with nothing else to do. My cell phone SD card was saturated with as much Afro-jazz and reggae tunes as I could download. And of course, I dutifully digested numerous texts devoted to Marcus Garvey's philosophies, and how ancient Egypt was such a glorious ebony civilisation. Needless to say, I was terrifically bored.

Then came the day the filmmaker and I went to a poetry event held at the cultural offices of a European embassy. He loved to cast his shadow at as many artistic gatherings as possible, because he knew he could always find an unfortunate captive audience to pour his hotep rhetoric on. The poor people never knew what hit them. I was always somehow persuaded to accompany him to such events where I would invariably end up swooning with embarrassment at his relentless pontificating. That particular day, he dressed himself in a dashiki of some shouting colour and implored me to dress as regally as possible, whatever that meant. He was going to read one of his innumerable, epic-sized poems and was practically vibrating with pride at the thought. He had managed to coax me to also recite some of my own verse and, unlike him, I was dreading the experience.

We showed up at the event well ahead of time and he quickly pounced on an unsuspecting pair of Europeans who had also arrived early. He wasted no time launching into a detailed description of his latest documentary. Its footage chiefly comprised of him talking to the camera about how profound a journey it had been for him to trace his family tree. I yawned on the pair's behalf. To occupy myself I decided to scrutinise the people around me. That proved not quite as stimulating as I had hoped, since they all appeared so generic as to have been mass produced in a single sweatshop. That is until my jaded eyes fell on an unusual young man standing alone in a corner, puffing deliberately on a cigarette. He surely knew smoking was prohibited in that space and he seemed to be waiting for someone to tell him to take his cigarette elsewhere. Strangely, no one did.

I watched him closely. Something in the way he smoked his cancer stick reminded me of an electric eel. His dreads were matted beyond repair and his faded blue jeans were so torn as to be shredded. Everything about his appearance was threadbare, everything except his eyes. They were at once reptilian and hypnotic. They were the kind of eyes that drew you in and never allowed you to erase them. He had a colossal quality about him and even from a distance I felt dwarfed. The textbook feminist in me told me I shouldn't, but I did anyway. Then, very unexpectedly, his eyes and mine collided and in that instant a startling vision of a teapot-shaped country consumed in unforgiving flames flashed through my mind.

I nervously looked away and moved closer to the filmmaker, who was by now busy expounding on the veracity of his theory that Jesus Christ was not a Palestinian Jew as so often thought, but in fact an African Hebrew. After too long a wait the event commenced, and I found myself quite perturbed by the sheer volume of self-styled poets clambering for an opportunity to stand up front and offload their incoherent ramblings on a bemused audience. Most of the poems were of the protest variety.

After what seemed like hundreds of bewildering recitals it came time for the filmmaker to share his verse. He stood up and strutted to the podium, resembling an inflated peacock in posture. He took a considerable amount of time pronouncing salutations and greetings before commencing his delivery. His poem turned out to be an extremely energetic, nearly thirty-minute-long homage to Negritude. When he eventually finished, he was swimming in sweat and the audience was panting with exhaustion. The applause that followed was so rapturous and enthusiastic, I suspected it had less to do with his poetic gifts and more with people thanking him for stopping. I took the podium after him. My recital was much less flamboyant than his, although still peppered with the obligatory salutes to African warrior queens such as Queen Nzinga and Yaa Asantewaa. I read haltingly from a tightly-clutched piece of handwritten paper, and made sure to avoid any chance of eye contact with anyone in the audience. I quickly scurried back to my seat even before I could breathe the last letter of my poem. The applause was indifferent, but I wasn't concerned.

The last person to recite poetry was the strange young man I had noticed earlier. His first words were, "No, I don't hate being black. I'm just tired of saying it's beautiful." An echo of Dambudzo Marechera, our country's most iconoclastic and most troubled writer. The filmmaker shifted uneasily next to me. The young man proceeded to launch into a recital that strongly reminded me of some surrealist poetry I had stumbled across in my readings.

My companion leaned over to me and whispered contemptuously in my ear, "What a sell-out. He's the type we didn't hesitate to eliminate during the liberation struggle."

"When you say 'we' who exactly are you referring to? You were born just after independence," I pointed out.

"Well, yes of course I was, but you know very well if I was there during that time, I would have been a very gallant guerrilla fighter, that clearly goes without saying," the filmmaker stated, sounding unconvinced.

As the odd young man wrapped up his poem to genuine appreciative applause from the audience, my companion suddenly shot up from his chair without warning and screamed, "Coconut!" at him.

The peculiar young man did not as much as miss a breath. "I would rather be that, than an utterly misguided propagator of prescribed identities such as yourself, good sir," he deftly responded.

I could see the tension dancing gleefully in the air. Unable to conjure up a sufficient retort, the filmmaker crumbled back into his chair, muttering futile obscenities under his breath. With the friction defused, the event came to an anti-climactic end. Uncharacteristically the filmmaker was quite anxious for us to leave immediately, but I was in no hurry to go home. I knew the nightmares that awaited me there. The other option of going with the filmmaker to his place of residence was just as unsavoury. I had seen the way his lascivious eyes watched my boyish body, and I knew I would certainly endure some form of carnal violation if I dared go home with him. Since I was not prepared for such an ordeal, I told him I would remain behind for a while and make the most of the free wine being served. He spent some time trying to persuade me to leave with him. We haggled over the issue for a few minutes, but his attempts were ultimately in vain. I was determined to stay and he eventually left defeated.

I never saw much of him after that, although I did bump into him some weeks ago in the city centre. He had grown astoundingly obese and was now driving a monstrosity of a luxury vehicle, purchased from the proceeds of working as a film propagandist for the ruling party. He proudly told me he was now the owner of three residential properties in the leafy northern suburbs of the city, each house inhabited by its own customarily married wife. He joked half-seriously that if I had been nice to him back then, he would have gladly paid bride price for me long ago, and I would now also be enjoying the good life, like his other wives. I told him I was sure I would have made a most difficult wife for him, and he should thank his alert ancestors he never entered a union with one as challenging as myself. He laughed at my statement and assured me a 'Big Man' such as himself could handle any type of woman. I quickly noticed the double entendre in what he said but decided not to challenge him on it, because I lacked intimate enough knowledge to be certain he was wrong. Although I richly suspected he was. After I had given him a false phone number, he drove off in his eyesore of a car.

My thoughts drifted back to the day when a much thinner and less polygamous version of him left me downing free red wine after a generally dismal poetry function. I stood by myself making sure to look as aloof and unapproachable as possible. I was completely uninterested in idle chatter or in any form of interaction, I just wanted to be left alone with my drink and troubled thoughts. I managed to close myself off so successfully from those around me that at one point I felt myself merging into the room's elegant wallpaper. Or maybe it was just the wine performing its magic on my brain. Either way, I was thoroughly enjoying my little solitary bubble when a pair of disquieting eyes suddenly loomed large in my line of vision. They belonged to the weird young man who had earlier been involved in a spat with the filmmaker.

My first instinct was to avoid his eyes and look as far away from them as possible, but then I told myself they were just eyes. I also possessed a pair after all and mine were just as fully functional, so what could be so sacred? With that thought, I proceeded to gaze as hard into his eyes as I could. He did the same. And so we stood there for what seemed an interminable second, staring sharply through each other. One watched the other looking into the other like two reflecting mirrors. It was a pivotal moment in which an unidentified object long lodged in both our psyches creaked audibly and began to turn. Perception rotated on its axis and tilted abnormally to the side. A revolution was abreast and its focal point seemed to be an area of grey matter, a place of blurred lines. The moment was shattered into scattering shards by the voice of the unusual young man. What had just preceded lay strewn around me in pieces too infinitesimal to bend down and collect. I suddenly felt like weeping for what had passed, and for what I knew was impending.

The strange young man's voice was like scissors. "May I borrow a cigarette…or two?" he asked rather politely.

Without a word I fished through my Lesotho-bought handbag and retrieved a box. I handed it to him and watched him pull out four cigarettes.

"You smoke Kingsgate. The politician's choice," he remarked, eyeing me quizzically.

I shrugged, mumbled something about aren't we all political animals in one way or the other and handed him a lighter. He muttered something along the lines of the reason why overthrowing the governmental system is proving impossible is because governments start at the interpersonal and family levels going up, and being as deeply entrenched as they are makes attempting to root them out a most impractical mission. I asked him if he was by any chance an anarchist, and he told me he found the idea of a state system to be just as oppressive as subscribing to some fashionable 'ism'. I informed him that I was a practising nihilist and he told me that was meaningless to him. As he lit his cigarette, I asked his name. He told me it was Pan. My eyebrow raised itself. After a moment I heard myself say, "Human nature is the true god in these pagan times we're living in," and he shuffled his hooves. We stood wordlessly for a lengthy moment, lost in the turmoil of our different contemplations, while time marched on in military fashion.

Then my voice discovered itself. "What else is there? What else exists in this mundane environment but boxes stacked upon boxes? Boxes shaped like coffins that one is compelled or coerced to fit into. All they do is decay the lives of those entombed within them. What else is there but rows upon rows of suffocating boxlike shapes stretched out never-endingly like a universe of unmarked graves? What else is there but the four corners of conformity and the prison cells of uniformity? Is there anything else in these fortified rooms we sleepwalk through, corpse-like, inhaling fear and exhaling submission? To exist on the fringe is only an imaginary dream when one is enclosed in the towering walls of an inescapable cubicle. There are no peripheries in spaces such as these, only centralised certainties. Doubt cannot find herself a room in a place such as this, not even as a tenant. The only way to break out is the way of the martyr, but who was pushed out of his mother's uterus to end up a willing sacrifice? We are a cowardly people by essence, so all we do is fold ourselves as neatly as possible and allow ourselves to be methodically packed in like the inanimate objects we are. Nothing changes. A symbolic freedom might appear comfortingly real, but when thrown in the mouth the sham taste of it is impossible to ignore. It lingers like the flavour of a liberation betrayed. Judas times and a life sentence of boxes, that is our reality. So tell me what else is there? What else but a gradual succumbing?"

Pan shook his head in anticipated disagreement. A blistering silence reigned while I waited for the baptism of his words. With a voice like hot coals he spoke, "My dear, we have gone beyond such trivialities. We require no collective courageous mentality to propel us to act, when desperation is the single battery that compels us to charge. With tattered garments, dishevelled faces and dilated pupils, we shuffle forward headed for a dilapidated destiny. The time of living in cages has long since said goodbye and vacated the premises, leaving us at liberty to crack the padlocks that once constrained us and spill out like a seething dark mass unattached to tomorrow. Moving in disjointed unison, humming haunting melodies from the days before the big bang, we cannot fail to notice the fallen idols scattered at our feet – they lie shattered and broken like our heroes' skulls. Our signals are so scrambled we clumsily fan out in every direction like the tentacles of an inebriated octopus. Kings abdicate thrones and lords abandon fiefdoms at the sight of our approaching horde. They come and cower at our feet, elite knees begging for small mercies, unaware that we are in fact Aztecs in working-class disguise. They watch in disbelief as we rip out their hearts raw and raise them to the sun – the only god that has not failed us thus far. We are not a spring; we are the coming of the dry season in its thirstiest form."

Little else was spoken between us after that exchange but we remained in close proximity until the function came to an end. The two of us made our exit simultaneously and our feet found themselves travelling in tandem. This seamless flow of motion was only interrupted when I decided to get into a taxi. Just before the taxi rattled off with me in it, he told me he would be in a particular area of the city gardens at noon the next day. He did not have a mobile phone so he would wait for me until dusk. I promised him I would show up and the vehicle began to move.

Now he is crouching on the floor across from me. He rocks back and forth like a scorned child while humming a vague tune. A stillborn atmosphere pervades the room. I close my eyes and succumb to the psychedelia of my dreams. I'm jolted out of sleep by a stinging slap on my face. I curse fiercely and spit at Pan's hovering face. I miss and he attempts to slap me again, on the other cheek this time. I dodge the impact and shove him ferociously. He teeters precariously like a colonial statue under violent assault from an angry post-colonial mob before he eventually topples over. He quickly springs back up with an unreadable expression on his face.

"Get up, let's go grab food and other necessities," he says briskly, throwing a too often worn black leather jacket onto his upper body.

I rise indignantly and clutch my purse. We walk outside and I notice that the women milling around the gate seem to have doubled in number even though it is still fairly early in the day. They are swarming like lusty queen bees, their honey on full display. One of the women has the most enormous breasts I have ever laid eyes on. They are the size of planets, and they dance around mischievously in the confines of her low-cut top with each movement she makes. Pan's eyes are as riveted on the woman's bosom as mine are. I think of the peas on my own chest and something inside me dampens.

We walk past the jovial old man who repairs shoes at appallingly low prices for a living, and the young man with a talkative face who sells cell phone airtime near the entrance to the block of flats, and we exchange greetings with both. The young man is gazing at Pan with a naked admiration that desperately needs to be clothed. I'm certain he saw him arriving with the French woman yesterday evening. We pass the abandoned high-rise building still far from complete a decade after its construction stalled due to faulty financing. A few metres ahead of us, three male vagrants huddle under a hulking *musasa* tree while partaking of some suspicious transparent liquid swimming in a plastic Coca-Cola bottle. Both of us hasten our steps as we pass them. One of the vagrants once grabbed my arm and refused to let go, loudly demanding sex as his ransom. Pan almost choked the intercourse-starved creature to death. The vagrants toast us drunkenly as we hurry past, but we do not acknowledge them.

We find our way to the nearby shopping centre where Pan is inundated with hollers of "Rasta!" and "Dread!" and an abnormally high amount of fist-bumping from the cluster of unemployed male youths who hang about the shops. He takes it in stride; he is used to this sort of attention. Inside the supermarket Pan wastes no time buying three bottles of a quite expensive brand of vodka and I splurge on a surprising amount of cigarettes and a couple of ciders. In the process of paying at the till, Pan jokes with the female till operator that he sorely misses shoplifting and she chuckles at this. I'm aware he is not actually joking because he has a pair of lighters in his pocket that he took and isn't intending to pay for. We leave the store and go to a fast-food place a few metres away. Pan orders a large vegetarian pizza and I order a small pizza with an overabundance of domesticated animal flesh on it. He throws me a disgusted look, but I simply shrug and blame my dietary sins on evolution.

After completing our shopping, we retrace our steps back to his flat arguing about the difference between culture and tradition, and the ways the two contribute to the patriarchal nature of our society. The debate gets so animated we end up loudly questioning each other's intellectual faculties in the street while people pass us and stare. Before reaching Pan's place, we make a detour into the abandoned building we passed earlier. As we walk through its gaping ground floor doorway, I decide there is something harrowing about the building's forlornness, something reminiscent of the traumatic edifice of youth.

The dimness inside is hellish. An image of Dante's Inferno explodes inside my thoughts. I shiver and nearly whisper the Lord's Prayer. I'm startled when a group of bats lying dormant in a corner of the unfinished roof suddenly flutter to life and begin to sail above our heads. I'm uneasy but Pan tells me to relax, apparently the bats are his kin and they are merely welcoming us. He has always considered himself something of a vampire, although more in a psychological rather than blood-drinking sense.

Disparate snatches of voice seep through the dejected walls and I momentarily feel as if I'm moving through a mausoleum awakening from its slumber. As we move further into the interior, the dizzying stench of stale urine reaches out and greets us enthusiastically. The sound of our shoes on the half-baked floor is disturbingly intrusive to my ears. Our destination is an inner room at the far end. The room is shockingly wide and my antenna immediately picks up an atmosphere of suppressed violence. A sprinkling of men with tomato-red eyes, chaotic hair and nothing-to-lose expressions sit on creaky chairs. As we enter, they watch us closely. Large plastic bags heaving with anonymous contents sit snugly on the ground around them. Also on the ground, close to their feet lies a naked woman. She is sprawled out awkwardly and I cannot help noticing the forest of silky midnight-coloured hair covering her vagina. Her body is as ripe and voluptuous as a summer fruit and she appears unconscious. The men pay her no attention but as I study her face, I recognise her. She is one of the sex workers who stand by the gate at Pan's block of flats. I wonder what has befallen her but am wise enough not to voice my curiosity.

Pan wastes no time explaining the purpose of our visit. I watch them listening to his words and nodding nonchalantly as he speaks. Pan proceeds to hand them a few weathered dollar notes and turns to me to ask if I also want something. I nod before taking some money out of my purse and handing it to him. He passes it on to the men. I'm slightly annoyed at the degree of protocol going on. It makes me feel like I'm trying to access a basic service in a government office. And I want to know what's wrong with the woman on the ground! But I maintain my composure and wait impatiently as one of the men takes his sour time lazily rummaging through a plastic bag. He finally pulls out some miniature bottles of an illicit cane spirit smuggled from a neighbouring country that is still recovering from a protracted civil war. This illegal spirit is apparently produced en masse in that country. One would think its citizens would have more pressing issues to attend to, like nation-building for instance, rather than devoting their time and resources to brewing toxic beverages. The bottles are handed to Pan and another bottle of a banned brand of cough syrup lands in my hands. We both thank our suppliers much too profusely before making a hasty retreat from the building. As we exit, I decide the scene in the room we have just left would have made for a most intriguing photograph.

We find ourselves back in Pan's flat where we deposit all our purchases on the unswept floor. We unburden our terrors and permit ourselves the luxury of uncoiling. Pan's rented four walls are a sanctuary where we can sit cordially alongside our devils. My fingers tinker with the typewriter. Pan starts playing deafeningly loud Bhundu Boys music from his laptop. The infectious sound of *jit* permeates the entire space, making my limbs want to gyrate and contort in rhythm with the pulsating beat. I take a few sips from my bottle of cough syrup. Pan starts to dance in the untamed feverish manner native to him. He is all flailing hands, twisting torso and reckless legs. His hair is a flock of crows in electric flight. The way he whirls with an air of such oblivious abandon makes me envious. I wish to be that loose, that unhampered, that close to nirvana. Instead, I settle more comfortably in my ennui, swallow my never-shed tears and gradually begin to mould.

I am aware that although my external world is a desert wasteland, my interior is a diseased swamp teeming with psychotic bacteria ever ready to inflame and infect all hope, all chance of revival. Recovery is an idealistic fantasy not worth dwelling on, so I shift my attention to Pan's writhing frame moving maniacally about the room. I am a creature resigned. Eventually Pan and I sit in uneasy silence. We avoid each other's soaked eyes and instead focus our pupils on unintended lessons somewhere in the distance. A shiver enters my spine and takes residence there. A shadow the colour of indigo descends and tinges the two of us with an awareness of the ominous things of life. The kinds of things that cannot be escaped or hammered out of the activity of one's inexorable brain activity. Things that consist of the cracking and shattering of one's tenuous hold on the stained glass of reality. Things ghoulish and gangrenous. Things that have made themselves a permanent home in the gut of my generation. Things that refuse to leave us be until our sadistic decay is complete and concretised. Disquieting things that resemble a pus-like apathy oozing from every pore of one's being. Things sickeningly pungent, the festering smell of which cannot be cleansed off or perfumed away. Things that have crystallised their rottenness at the core, things seemingly impossible to purify.

"Vanity of vanities, all is vanity," Pan mutters.

I sigh before taking a long swig from my bottle. I watch a fly roaming about our heads. My body feels like lead. The music has now transformed into a Chopin composition and my waxy ears approve.

"Paradigm shifts are improbable constructs, aren't they? In truth stagnation reigns," I say to nobody in particular and Pan grunts.

The jarring sound of a 1970s punk song suddenly joins Chopin. Pan's cell phone is ringing. I halt Chopin in mid-note and listen as Pan answers the phone. He speaks in his 'lover boy' voice to the person on the other end, a voice that feels like warm fingers caressing lonely skin. The person he is speaking to is the Russian woman who pays his rent. She lives in St Petersburg with her husband – a wealthy industrialist – but she visits our teapot-shaped country often, due to her work as an art curator. Whenever she comes, the two of them invariably meet for sexual purposes. Their first encounter was a year and a half ago at an exhibition where the chemistry between them was immediate. She is quite some years older than him, but she is so striking a woman to behold that the small matter of age makes not an ounce of difference. She found him a place to rent about a year ago. This is the same place we are in now. I once asked him if he loves his Russian and he replied that he finds her extremely beautiful. She calls him weekly without fail and in this particular conversation I gather that she will be in the country in two months. He tells her he is delighted to know she will be around soon, he has been missing her terribly, almost to the point of nervous breakdown, and he is craving to hold her in his yearning arms again. There is something affected about his tone as he speaks to her. They talk for half an hour and as the conversation winds down, Pan implores her to send him some extra money as soon as she can. He has been suffering from an undisclosed illness and needs the money for hospital consultations and to buy medication. Pan appears in impressively good health to me, but I cannot be the judge of the condition of another's immune system. They end the conversation with protestations of unbridled love before she hangs up.

I throw Pan a quizzical look and he blurts out a sharp "What?!" My eyes swivel from his annoyed face to a pair of flies copulating on the windowsill. I tune out of my surroundings and become engrossed in my cocktail of cider and cough syrup. I'm sure Pan is drowning in his own sea of vodka and poisonous alcohol, but I don't bother to check. Strange apparition-like forms begin to manifest in my line of vision. They are the colour of infrared and ultraviolet and they perform a languid uncoordinated dance for my viewing pleasure. I'm entranced by their mesmeric beauty and stretch out my right hand to stroke them lovingly, but they evaporate at the threat of touch. As soon as my hand falls away, they quickly reappear in the form of majestic nebulae floating seductively in front of my eyes. They would look so pretty if they were brightly oiled on canvas. Soon the nebulae are joined by fiery polka-dots orbiting nothing spectacular. These little circular forms exude an incandescence that begs to be worshipped. A riderless purple unicorn gallops past and I hoot like the delighted owl that I am. A blood-drenched rosary zooms in and out of focus and I listen to myself pray in tongues.

Somewhere in the room, an existential earthquake rocks the centre. I hold on tightly to the ground of my being while fervently hoping the roof of the mind does not cave in. Something crashes with a shrieking loudness. A crystal ball lies stricken on the floor in flickering shards that wink mischievously at my nervous condition. I wish to vomit out the bitterness, but the bile mingles too closely with the bloodstream. To purge out the cursed angel is to sever ties with the breath of life itself. My spine slithers under my skin and a love like a forked tongue licks my face. There is nothing to be gained, only mountains of loss.

An image of my deceased paternal grandmother emerges out of the still air. Her eyes are fixated on my rottenness and I feel the irresistible pull of uprooted family trees. She is calling me without uttering a word and I feel powerless to resist her forces. She is dressed in her *svikiro* robes. Billowing black fabric shrouds her body like mist over Mount Nyangani. I tell Pan that my grandmother has visited again and he tells me to keep quiet, he is engrossed in a very engaging conversation with his dead father and I'm disturbing them. I greet my grandmother softly and respectfully with eyes cast down, but she shakes her head disapprovingly. I have disappointed her by consistently refusing to answer when I am summoned. I ask for forgiveness for what seems like the thousandth time, but she does not respond. Her obstinacy is an indictment I cannot bear and I begin to whimper despairingly. Pan laughs heartily at something his father has just said, and my grandmother inches forward, a subterranean look in her eyes.

My grandmother died when I was fifteen. I remember a bespectacled teacher from the boarding school I attended pulling me aside and gravely relaying the news to me. I recall him watching me closely as the words sank in, probably waiting for an anticipated outburst of violent grief but it was not forthcoming. I had not known my paternal grandmother well enough to feel anything but a curious rocking motion inside my head when I heard she was no more. The news destabilised me for, at most, a minute before my normal state of numbness resumed.

What I knew of her was that she was a Head Nurse at a rural district clinic, she possessed remarkably long and thick natural hair, and she was a *svikiro*, a spirit medium, in her spare time. The one time we spoke for longer than the customary greetings, she swiftly launched into a lengthy explanation about the parallels between Shona spirituality and Christian theology, as well as those between the sacrificial martyr deaths of the messianic figures of Nehanda Nyakasikana and Jesus Christ.

Growing up, I heard unsavoury rumours that she had deserted her children, my father included, when they were still young, only to reappear when they were fully functional adults, and such talk always made me survey her with a wary eye. Her marriage to my paternal grandfather had not lasted many years and she had never sought to remarry after that. I remember her being a very inward, taciturn woman who seemed to take great pains to insulate herself from the emotional level of human contact. I think I am certainly her granddaughter in this regard. I did not attend her funeral, I spent that day playing truant from my Mathematics and Accounting classes. A sociopathic gift for erasure soon rubbed all thought of my extinguished grandmother from my consciousness and life lumbered on, wooden as ever. Now whenever I used the term *Gogo* or Grandma, I referred to the industrious and admirably self-sufficient mother of my mother who still roamed the earth, albeit on incurably arthritic legs. And so with time, my paternal grandmother's significance diminished further and further, until she had shrunk to the size of a subatomic particle in my memory. And life crawled on, slimy as ever.

And then four years to the day when she went to become an ancestor, she appeared again. So unexpectedly, after such a chasm of time. It was a day when I had forfeited all pretence of meaningful activity and elected to spend my time getting my hair braided by the family hairdresser in the comfort of my parents' upstairs living room. The extensions I was using were imported from Dubai, courtesy of my mother. Appearance was ultimate, of course. The hairdresser was a talkative, gossipy woman a few years older than me, with three children all below the age of six. Although she was a generally amiable person who was skilled at her craft, she also had something of the nymphomaniac about her. She loved to talk about men, all things masculine seemed to thrill and enthral her to no end. Her voice would get husky and uncomfortably moist as she talked about the litany of males she had bedded, and the unattainable ones she nonetheless still heavily lusted after. The three fathers of her children had all left her for other women, but she seemed not to mind. She was perpetually on the prowl for the next penis to conquer and seemed to revel in this predatory pursuit.

On the day in question she was rambling on as usual about this and that fellow while she dealt with my hair. I couldn't stop yawning. Midway through the braiding process, she started lamenting about how shocking it was that she had somehow managed to reach her age without tasting a white man. That was an abomination in her opinion and certainly needed to be rectified. Not sure how to console her, I simply listened to her chattering voice droning on. Soon my eyelids gave up and started to droop, and my head began to lose balance. I was dozing off. I tried to struggle against the tranquilising seduction of sleep, and in my attempt to pull back its heavy curtains I forced my eyes to open wide. That is the moment I saw my buried grandmother standing slightly to the side, in front of me.

I was so startled, my body jerked with such ferocity the hairdresser was momentarily silenced. She asked me if I was alright, had she twisted my hair too tightly? I shook my head and croaked that I had been bitten by an insect and was startled by the bite's sting. She seemed to find my response satisfactory and started to tell me about the day she was stung by a wasp, back in her primary school days.

"Oooh, the pain was so sharp, I'll never forget it," I heard her say, as though through static.

My eyes were riveted on Grandmother looming there, her hair soaring in that brazen way I remembered from childhood. For some reason I suddenly felt acutely nostalgic, but for what, I could not pinpoint. Grandmother was holding out an ochre-coloured wrap cloth, her branchlike arms stretched almost to the tip of my nose. Her eyes were a silent plea for me to receive it, but my hands had turned to granite. She stood there for a resilient length of time waiting for me to accept what was offered, before cool saltless tears gradually began to stain her archaeological features. I wanted to look away, to redirect my sight elsewhere but I couldn't. The empty space where her heart used to pump when she lived was breaking, fracturing, irreversibly, excruciatingly, and I was the culprit. Her lips were moving, and in the silences they produced, I could hear the wailing of distant worlds. Her skin rose in a whirlwind like drunken dust, ascending ever higher until it disappeared into the nightly heights beyond. I watched her tremble with uncompressed fury and I knew I had trespassed into a Hades of sorts. Her wrath burst into a multiplication of dark crow wings that flapped maniacally out of the window with the promise of vengeful returns.

All was calmness and solid reality again. Relief flooded me in streams of sanity that I drank from thirstily. I could not fathom what I had just witnessed, but I was glad it had died as quickly as it had been born. I was convinced nothing of the sort would ever occur again, it had just been a schizophrenic ripple on an otherwise serene surface, certainly never to be repeated. I was wrong. Grandmother returned three days later. I was lazing in my bedroom at nightfall, surfing the internet in hopes of stumbling upon some much-needed stimulus. There was none. I felt an iron breeze strike my skin and looked up. It was Grandmother. She was dressed in a straw ensemble I could not quite understand. She was holding out a wounded white lion cub, but again I refused to accept her gift. When Grandmother realised she had again been rejected, she bared her decayed fangs and her eyes began to flash in a manner better suited to lightning. She started to utter words like rusty nails in human flesh, as she slowly advanced towards my immobilised frame.

I was brimming with fear and soon a shattering cry spilled from my throat. The first person to come bounding into my room was my younger sister; she took one look at my petrified face and screamed for my parents to come. At the arrival of my sister, Grandmother promptly crumbled into a heap of ashes that seemed to blink at me with malicious eyes. When my parents appeared, followed closely by the housekeeper clutching a Bible, I told them I had had a bad vision but it was gone now. I was too terrified to reveal it was Grandmother. My parents stood around helplessly, unsure of what could be done. My mother's expensive face looked its poorest, and my father decided I should take sleeping pills that night. My sister had her arms around my shoulders, attempting to comfort me. Eventually the housekeeper offered to say a prayer, and everyone except me bowed their heads and shut their eyelids. The housekeeper proceeded to unleash a most theatrical prayer of pentecostal proportions that I found quite entertaining. I giggled throughout her godly exhortations and Christly incantations, and when she said the final amen – there were quite a number prior, mind you – I clapped delightedly. They all looked at me with eyes that told of an uneasy shock creeping in. My father instructed my sister to go fetch a bottle of sleeping pills from my parents' medicine cabinet, and after swallowing two, I fell into a graveyard sleep. But Grandmother did not go away.

Her visits became more frequent as the days and weeks trundled on, and the nature of these appearances became ever more insistent and urgent. She usually showed up when the sun had gone to sleep for the day, at the time when a crisp stillness sharpened the air. She always arrived when I was home unwinding, and she always caught me at my most unguarded. I started trying to anticipate or pre-empt when she would come, but this was always in vain. Grandmother had a way of deeply unnerving me with her sudden arrivals, a way that caused an uncontrolled anxiety to sprout and grow out of the cracked mirror of my being. Soon, I began to both expect and dread Grandmother's familiar deadness bearing down on me in the most relentless of manners. I could not wipe her off, she was the stubborn stain no decorated detergent could clear. Her spectre was a shape-shifting array of alarming guises meant to contort my limits to their snapping point.

At times she would hold out piles of rotting dead fish whose unearthly odour and glassy staring eyes would drive me to the point of nausea. There was the day she came riding on a salivating lioness that gazed at me with such entrenched starvation I screamed so sharply my vocal cords complained. Sometimes she took on a serpentine form that chilled me with its cunning deviance, other times she sat cross-legged on the floor and performed heavy rituals I could not pretend to comprehend. On some occasions, she would carefully write her indecipherable thoughts in the air using her finger. She would write in the most aesthetically perfect calligraphy imaginable. She would offer me strings upon strings of beads in multiple colours while instructing me to abstain from the plastic fashions of the day. And there were the dozens of papyrus scrolls she started to bring me every time she visited. She strongly urged me to read these scrolls, despite the fact that they were written in an ancient language from beneath, a language too complex for me to decode. I remember Grandmother draped in blankets intently stoking the waning fire dying inside me. She offered me a compass once, it pointed nowhere existent but somehow showed the way.

In the beginning, I would resolutely ignore Grandmother's overtures and her gibberish talk, but as her visits became more sustained and predictable, my resolve softened, and I gradually began to unlock my padlocked doors to allow her a measure of entry. I started thanking her graciously for all the varying gifts she unfailingly brought every time she came. I also noticed that her speech was not as nonsensical as I had earlier dismissed it to be, and soon began engaging in rich insightful discussions with her about everything from metaphysics to the science of rainmaking. She had such an expansive mind and I was slowly lured into an irresistible alliance governed by her invisible intellect and abilities.

I did not much care that the people I lived with would cast furtive anxious glances my way and shift their bodies unhappily whenever I spoke to Grandmother. I had explained the whole situation to my parents after her third visit and now whenever I conversed with her in the presence of my family members, other relatives, or the domestic staff, they would all maintain a stiff sober silence until my conversation with Grandmother was over. I took this as a sign of respectful honour for the depth of our discourses. The more absorbed I became in Grandmother, the less interest I had in those around me. The common cord that supposedly connected me to them began to seem less authentic and more contrived with each new sunrise. They all appeared so mundane and routine compared to the colossus I was now regularly confronting in the spectacle of my reawakened foremother. They were fading in relevance in a very rapid fashion.

Sometimes I would glimpse my mother or sister, their faces ravaged with unmasked horror and their cheeks sparkling with shimmering tears as they watched me from a distance. Other times I would notice my father, his accomplished features knotted in bundles of tension and despondency so severe I longed to untie them for him, although I lacked the knowledge of how to do so. The housekeeper would study me with a disgusted disdain that prickled my skin. She took to keeping a bottle of church-purchased holy water near enough to sprinkle herself and her surroundings whenever she encountered me in the house or in the yard. I ignored her antics. The gardener would simply stare at me with such a look of confused curiosity that I would find myself feeling slightly embarrassed, but only slightly.

My mother soon got into the habit of ushering me into my bedroom and locking the door from outside when family friends or relatives visited. But I wasn't offended. In fact, it was quite alright because Grandmother hated guests. I would occasionally pick up snatches of talk between my parents and some other people who paid too many courtesy calls for it to still be courteous. Phrases such as "we should take her to this-and-that faith healer or traditional healer" and "no, what she needs is thorough medical treatment" would bubble down to me as I swam with Grandmother. Grandmother loved the water, she said it was her shrine. It was also her source of replenishment, the place where she stocked up on her mysterious supplies. Grandmother would bring me the river, its precious waters contained within her amorphous hands, and I would wade in enthusiastically, ready to soak up its secrets. I soon discovered the river was a friend. It housed amphibious entities that greatly enjoyed unfurling their vast landscapes of waterborne wisdom for the feeding of my famine. I drank in their knowledge with a thirst that remained perennially parched. Some days Grandmother would come clothed in the electrifying neon-blue waters of the caves of Chinhoyi and I would not hesitate to delve into their haunted pools, mermaid-like.

As Grandmother intensified into an ever-evolving necessity in the corridors of my consciousness, the naturally fragile link I had always maintained with my environment began to loosen and slacken further until I felt myself almost entirely dissociated. Then came the day

I was seated awkwardly in a large claustrophobic room in a (mental) institution of higher learning. It was my first – and excruciatingly dismal – attempt at acquiring a university education. I was valiantly fighting to focus my concentration on what the female lecturer with a hideous perm was preaching, but I was of course failing fantastically. In the process of this quiet struggle, I felt a thing stir within the recesses of my inner ear. It was a faint pounding sound, a dull ache too subtle to be medicated. My body tensed as I waited and listened. Something was afoot.

As the sound became more audible, it took on a musical quality. I located it somewhere between a prehistoric chant and the hungry impatience of flapping vulture wings. The air suddenly became moist and I felt myself drenched by titanic forces. A beastly spasm ripped through my system with such urgency I had to sharply cough it out. A few of the other students turned their heads to see what the noise was about, but the face that stared back at them was as straight and uncreased as if it had been ironed. Nothing more transpired in the next minutes. I began to tell myself what I had just experienced was a mere fleeting episode of no importance that deserved to be languidly brushed off the jacket of my thoughts. I should have sensed the tap was about to start gushing.

A disturbing silence blanketed the room as I gazed at the lecturer mouthing words I could not decipher. She sounded like she was speaking a foreign tongue I hadn't mastered. And then I noticed the impossibly large crow perched on her left shoulder. It was glaring at me with eyes the colour of burnished gold. I gasped. In a corner of the room, an enormous crocodile swished its tail lazily while watching me intently. It was still dripping river water. Something inside my mind began to quiver just as I heard a lion unleash a ravenous roar nearby. The male student sitting next to me now possessed the head of a rabid dog. He was baring his teeth in a most unsettling way as he stared at me. I froze. All I could do was stare back at him with fear.

Then a familiar voice called my name. It was Grandmother. I searched frantically for her reassuring presence, but the sight of her brought little comfort. Right in the middle of the room grew a colossal tree, the revered tree of liberation. Grandmother swung from it helplessly. Her neck was decorated with the tightened noose of a rope, and her eyes kept rolling back in their sockets in a most unnatural manner. From the way she dangled, it was apparent she had been lynched. In one hand she held a hunting spear, in the other an antique rifle. The warrior had somehow been conquered. She was calling to me without uttering a word, pleading for me to assist her, begging to be rescued but I just sat there uselessly, strange sounds emanating from my throat. Her body began to thrash and flail in a sickening manner. It was too grotesque to watch, this last desperate attempt to cling to existence, so I looked away. I couldn't bear to watch her leave, knowing I was powerless to stop the process. Unexpectedly, a blood-curdling shriek tore from the tree and raced to slap me madly in the face. My head snapped up and I glimpsed Grandmother pointing her rifle at my chest.

In the moment she pulled the trigger, a sensation of drowning filled my nose, ears and mouth. I was being suffocated by too much air, too much life. I struggled to release myself from my evolutionary entanglements, but the physical part of me was far too cemented. I felt hot hands encircle my throat and begin to squeeze the stability out of me. Everything was shattered, cracked, broken. All things became sharp gleaming pieces of a dropped mirror scattered on the floor, rendered incapable of constructing a coherent image. And those damned hands kept on squeezing the foundation out of me. All I could do was crawl and scream…call and scream…fall and dream. My surroundings turned a blurry colour. I could hear faces hovering and I smelt commotion in the southern air. My eyes were too discordant to make any serious sense of the tune playing around me, so I gave up trying to comprehend. I felt myself descend down a steep waterfall and imagined I was a tourist who had unexpectedly slipped over the edge of the Mosi-oa-Tunya. The sensation was both catastrophic and comforting. I flung my arms out as far as I could and let myself parachute down to my distorted destination.

When my focus returned I was in a familiar place, the backseat of my father's Mercedes. He was driving and my mother was on the passenger side. "She has her own car, what's she doing in his?" I wondered petulantly. None of them heard my question and neither answered. The vehicle was moving uncharacteristically fast. My father was usually a very careful driver, but something was oddly reckless about his driving today. Maybe he has started drinking again, I mused. I wanted to scold him about the obvious dangers of driving while intoxicated but my voice refused to rally. I sighed inwardly and chose not to think about where we might be going. I was too weary to think.

After a length of time, the car pulled into a neat driveway leading to a sprawling, single-story building painted the colour of bile. The building looked so sullen I immediately felt sorry for it. When we stepped out of the car, my mother quickly moved to put her hand in mine. This gesture of closeness surprised me and I glared at her glamorous features suspiciously. There was something funereal about our movements as all three of us walked to the entrance. I didn't ask what this place was, I didn't care to know. A sweetly pungent scent of raw animal skin wafted past my nostrils and I found it quite pleasant. I asked my mother if she could smell it too, but her only response was to tighten her grip on my hand. My father's expensive-shirted back walked ahead of us, businesslike as usual. I wanted to compliment him on how impressive he looked – how impressive he always looked – but my voice silenced itself. The glass doors led into a drab reception area that reminded me of transparent objects self-destructing. The whole place was far too clinical for my liking. I preferred my spaces infested and inflamed. The heavy-breasted woman behind the large, chipped desk wore a monotonous uniform of sorts. She had the face of a religious fanatic and I immediately decided I didn't like her.

"Gods are really only man-made entities for your information," I blurted out spitefully in her direction, but she seemed not to take notice of my blasphemy.

Her attention was focused on my parents who were saying some unintelligible things to her. Now and again, they would gesture at me rather emphatically, and she would nod and murmur agreeably. Watching her, I concluded that this woman was not only a fundamentalist, she was also condescending and arrogant, and therefore she was little more than a monstrosity in my estimation. I glared at her hatefully as my parents continued to make what sounded like serious arrangements with her. Why they were even wasting their valuable time conversing with this base woman was beyond me.

From the corner of my eye, I spied a familiar form standing not too far away. Grandmother still had the rope around her neck, but now it hung limp like a flaccid organ. She, however, stood very erect and still, the way a tree would stand just as it was about to be engulfed within the roar of a bushfire. There was a peculiar expression of panic on her face and I wondered what was worrying her. There was no attempt at communication from her side, so I sighed sadly and turned my attention back to my parents and the detestable woman behind the desk. My parents had mysteriously acquired pens and they were both methodically signing strange sheets of paper in a manner I found boring. I yawned pointedly but no one took heed.

I was about to complain that I didn't appreciate being ignored, when my father pulled out his bulging wallet and handed the unpleasant woman an inordinate wad of money. I couldn't help wondering what the transaction was for. What business could this uncouth woman possibly have with my parents? I glared at her with naked contempt, but she seemed careful to avoid locking eyes with me.

I heard my mother say, "We've paid extra so we expect her to be treated well. We won't tolerate abuse of any sort," in her firmest voice. What was she talking about? There was more buzzing talk of the number of visitors allowed and visiting times, but I chose not to follow the conversation. Whatever they were discussing was making my temples ache, and I decided I simply wanted to go home and make use of my bed. As I was about to make this fact known, my mother suddenly and unexpectedly bundled my stiff body up in her arms in a clumsy hug that lasted longer than was necessary. When she thankfully released me, I saw wetness on her cheeks and noticed her face uncharacteristically showing its age. I wondered what was wrong with her today but didn't bother to ask. My father's eyes were drunk-red as he patted my shoulder reassuringly. His face was the crumpled handwritten page discarded by a frustrated writer. They said little else before turning and leaving me to the mercies of the repugnant woman in a mediocre uniform of sorts.

Not a wave rippled the air. She came round from behind the desk, a cheap plastic smile on her face, and held out her hand. I recoiled and resolved never to uncoil. She said something about taking me to my room, and I asked her why my parents would book me into such a tasteless hotel. She shrugged and started walking briskly. I found my legs following hers. She led me down a number of melancholy corridors covered with doors. An image of boarding school invaded my mind. Odd shouts, shrieks and mutterings from unidentified sources accompanied our short walk. We finally stopped in front of D7. The upper part of its door had a rectangular barred section through which one could look from either inside D7 or from outside it. A set of keys was quickly produced and the door swung open to reveal a room the size of a matchbox furnished with a single, steel, unblanketed bed and a tiny sink in the corner. The whole scene was pitiful to say the least.

I loudly exclaimed to the woman in a uniform of sorts that I deserved to be better accommodated, but she replied that this would have to do for now. Seething, I declared I had no intention of staying in this hovel. She told me I had no choice, and I retorted that I was never in a powerless position in any situation. Her face wore an outfit of irritation as she told me to please cooperate, but I shook my head petulantly. I instructed her to phone my parents immediately and was informed that would not be possible. I hollered that I was being abducted, and she told me if I didn't quieten down, she would have to summon help. Before I could protest further, our standoff was rather rudely finalised when she suddenly and roughly shoved me into the room, and hurriedly locked the door before I could orient myself with what had just happened. Once I was safely imprisoned, her face peered at me through the miniature bars as her grating voice said someone would come attend to me soon. She also told no one in particular her name, and that she hoped we would become good friends over time. And then she left.

I stood in that little cell, feeling not quite right. There was a rat in the corner of the room, watching me sceptically. It had Grandmother's eyes. She hadn't abandoned me and I was genuinely grateful. I began to advance towards the rodent in an effort to make contact, but it darted away as soon as I moved. Tears that smelled like the ocean overwhelmed my eyes, and I shuddered down onto the uncarpeted floor. I was jolted back to grimness by the sound of the door creaking open. A young woman in a certain sort of medical uniform entered. She carried a tray with food I knew I had no appetite for. She attempted to make friendly conversation, but my response was a venomous snake. After waiting for a while, she told me she would not force me to eat, but I had no choice but to drink the pills in the tiny cup she was holding out. Refusal to take the pills would result in quite unpleasant consequences for me, she stated rather cheerily. I glared at her and weighed my options. I knew I had none, so I reached out for the little cup and reluctantly swallowed its contents while hissing foul curses at the waiting woman's ancestors under my breath. She pretended not to hear and took the tray with a sunny smile as she informed me she would be back soon. I told her not to bother returning, but she paid me no attention as she glided out.

Whatever was in those pills wasted no time beckoning me into the inviting folds of an enveloping darkness. I felt myself fading, erasing, vanishing into the coolness of a massive black blanket I wished not to flee from. But before disappearing completely, I witnessed myself being serenaded by a figure similar to Biggie Tembo. He composed and sang a most sedating lullaby while standing on my bed. The sound of the song was like refreshing balm on the rotting wound of my psyche, even my maggots were momentarily transfixed. As I listened, I knew full well my doppelganger waited moodily for me outside the gates of this godforsaken institution. I also knew she would wait and weary and wait but I would not reappear. I was reduced to the stuff of dungeons now, such was my fate. Somewhere, the lullaby turned into an anguished cry and I dropped into a yawning blackness with the deepest of thuds.

When I unfortunately fumbled back into the light, I found existence had metamorphosed itself into a jarring ritual of imposed activity. Life became an interaction of nerves. I vividly remember the tepid triple meals a day that were an insult to swallow. The baffling sessions with state university-educated psychiatrists which always left one feeling more fractious than before. The cold deathly baths that left more grime than they cleansed. The regular bruising boxing matches with semi-skilled staff. The outcomes of these fights were almost always inconclusive. The dreadful visits from edgy family members who spoke to you as if the world had ever been normal. The ghastly medication. The bloody, gruesome, mutilating solitude. The gradual disintegration of Grandmother into eight billion grains of the blackest, heaviest sand. "For dust you are and to dust you shall return…" The dozens upon dozens of fellow zombies shuffling unseeingly beside one, devouring themselves from the inside.

We were a lost and forgotten tribe, wandering aimlessly with no Moses to guide us. There were those who took lithium, there were others who tried to scream and scratch the affliction out, and there were still others who were resigned to a deafening muteness. The diseases of our thoughts had us clamped by the throat. The battle to be considered sane was a deflating, degrading one. We tried never to look into one another's eyes; the shame cut too deep. We mumbled and rambled to ourselves and shared private laughs with our ghosts. We hauled ourselves up each day and tried to master the philosophy of why really we had been born. We knew what we were – desolate pariahs, but our tears refused to weep for our lot.

Life was a stinging whirl of solitary sojourns in the midst of the myth of professional psychological power. Pretence was the easiest way to slip through the cracks undetected, hence many of us learned to hide, fake, conceal, imitate, ape, anything to leave. Quite a few succeeded. These were the ones who carried their safely-stashed baggage of lunacy with them into the unsuspecting outside. For those that remained behind, there was only that maddening howl in one's mind that never stopped piercing, that never ceased inflicting savage injury. It aimed for the softest spot and maimed the useful part. It drained all the health out of one's being, leaving dregs in its wake. It razed and ravaged, ruining even the foundations one was rooted in. Such was the dismal meal fate had chosen to serve on its platter and one had no option but to ingest.

I generally kept to myself in this warped environment since I felt none of the individuals around had anything of value to offer. I did practically everything on my own and barely uttered a word unless speech was absolutely critical. My silence and reserve became the protective cloak I daily shrouded myself with. Then came the day I was seated outside on a bench with a pencil and a sketchpad, absently attempting to draw my surroundings. We were encouraged to practise such type of 'art therapy' but I hardly found it healing. Still, it helped to ward off the monotony so I did it regularly.

As if from nowhere, a youthful creature came and sat beside me. His hair was a field of short dark spikes jutting up like upturned nails. His build was awkward, as if his body had tried and failed to wrest itself from the clutches of adolescence, and he wore the most elaborate horn-rimmed glasses I had ever laid eyes on. The air he exuded was both manic and moody. He promptly asked me what I was sketching, and before I could reply, he enquired if I was a dancer. I stared at him in confusion as he explained that I had the body of a ballerina, svelte and fluid. He told me he was a fierce lover of ballet and wondered if I was as passionate about it as he was. Before I could reply, he immediately delved into a lengthy monologue about the urgency of the creative moment within the artist. I found his thoughts so usefully brilliant, I couldn't resist converting my sketchpad into a notepad, and automatically started jotting down some of what he said. He didn't seem to mind this but instead spoke even more profoundly on his subject matter for the next hour, while I listened raptly and captured what I could of the hailstones flying down furiously at me from the sky of his mind. Then abruptly, he stopped and sat unnervingly still, staring into nothingness. I was dazed by this sudden and unexpected revolution, and quietly waited for the return of the status quo, but he remained as mute as the voices from a graveyard.

I eventually retrieved my capacity for speech and ventured to ask him if he was some sort of teacher by profession. He shook his head rather deliberately. A philosopher, then? He grunted in the negative. Then what was he, I probed in exasperation. He explained that he was in the process of completing his Masters in World Literature. I told him that was impressive and he asked why.

"I can only imagine the limitless wealth of books and writings you're exposed to. I envy you," I said wistfully.

"For a mad girl your brain seems to function rather sensibly," he remarked.

I informed him that I wasn't mad. I was quite the opposite actually. He simply raised his eyebrow. I proceeded to ask him why he wasn't busy working on his Masters somewhere in the hallowed halls of academia, why he was wasting his valuable time in this psychological dumpsite we both found ourselves in?

His answer: "I keep telling them I'm not insane, but they've made up their wayward minds that mine is a case of the deranged. It's true that my typewriter tells me things, significant things. It has a pontiff's voice and its language of choice is Latin. They tell me I don't have a typewriter. Are they mad? Then what did I use to write such classic works as *Two Thousand Seasons, Crime and Punishment, Ulysses* and *The Metamorphosis*? Was it not through the force of my beloved typewriter that these marvellous texts were penned? I know the establishment is behind this. They cannot stomach the extent of my mastery and command of the written word, of language. It's simply because I put them all to shame that I'm being persecuted. They say I have delusions of grandeur. Me? Certainly not. Does my greatness not speak for itself? My typewriter tells me to ignore these envious enemies and soldier on with my work. I agree with it. In fact, I already have ideas for my next book. It's going to be a masterpiece entitled *Black Sunlight*. Its first lines begin, 'Through the open window. The fucking window, a slashing wind blows…'" His voice trailed off.

I stared at him sympathetically and debated within myself how best to respond, if at all a response was necessary. I decided to allow him the liberty of his illusions and restrained my tongue. We sat in an atmosphere of amiable companionship for an extended period, and eventually parted rather warmly for two individuals who had no prior knowledge of each other before that particular encounter. He became the nearest thing to a friend I had at that concentration camp for the mind. He nicknamed me Mupengo and I returned the favour by christening him Benzi, both meaning 'mad person' in ChiShona. We would meet as often as was permissible and spend timeless hours discussing everything, from the poetry of T.S. Eliot and Christopher Okigbo to the ongoing obliteration of indigenous culture by the ravages of contemporary life. There were conversations about the myth of socialism in the post-independence African state versus the neo-liberal tendencies of its ruling elite.

Benzi promised that when we got out, he would take me to a field of flame lilies and paint me in all my superb glory. I said only if it would be a nude portrait in the classical tradition. I remember his glasses glinting brightly at these words. We urged, pushed and goaded each other to write, and this meant every time we met, there was always something new and terrifying to share. Our hunger for words, whether spoken, written or thought, was so voracious it threatened to swallow us both whole. Uncannily, the two of us shared a natural inclination for prose-poetry; it flowed out of our pens as easily as mucus falling from the nostrils of a toddler on a wintry day. We vowed to one another that once we left the confines of our present incarceration, we would labour to get our work published because a pair of unheralded poets such as ourselves simply deserved to be read. Benzi would speak at length about how he couldn't wait to resume working on his dissertation whose focus was the intersections between francophone and anglophone post-colonial African literature, and I would probe for more information on the subject in the basic French I knew. He had a phrase he would randomly repeat at the oddest moments: "My mother was a man in a dress. She was all testicles." I couldn't quite ascertain whether this statement was sexist or not, but I never ventured to quiz it.

The idealism we infused each other with in those pathetic days proved to be more medicinal than any of the therapies administered at that prison of an institution. Grandmother's presence continued to recede further into the background until all that remained of her diminished form was a mere speck on the periphery of my vision. The psychiatrists started noting what they called my 'increasing reengagement with reality', while Benzi's bouts of frenzy and catatonia also appeared to stabilise drastically. The two of us clung fiercely to the sense of solidity we gained from our lonely companionship as the lunatic days dragged on unchecked.

Then came the afternoon when separation came urgently knocking. Benzi and I were seated under the coolness of our favourite tree, debating about which poetic form was more sublime between the sonnet and haiku, when a nurse approached us and told me my parents were waiting.

"But I wasn't expecting a visit from them today," I said, confused.

"They're not visiting, they're here to take you home. You've been discharged," the male nurse stated matter-of-factly.

"Oh, I have? What about him?" I blurted out, pointing to Benzi.

It was the nurse's turn to look confused. "Him?" he asked, casting Benzi an uncertain glance.

"Hasn't he been discharged too?" I enquired hopefully.

"No," was the nurse's curt reply before briskly walking away.

I turned to Benzi and saw the same terror that I knew was etched on my own face mirrored on his. Without a word spoken, we embraced with a ferocity filled with endings that could not be bandaged or medicated, an embrace of the damaged and doomed. Our tears mingled and dried, trickled and cried, as one held on to the other as if our minds depended on it. To some extent they did. When we finally relinquished our hold, we promised to stay in contact, and I assured him he would receive regular visits from me, although we were both convinced he would also be released soon after. We accordingly made plans to meet on the great outside. As I stood up to go, the atmosphere appeared suddenly assaulted by a violent bleakness the colour of overcast days, and I almost choked on the hopelessness of it all. With a final wave that seemed to stagger under the weight of its own grief, I left him and went to those biologically responsible for me.

Once again, I found myself in the backseat of one of my father's cars as he drove me carefully to a jail of a different kind, a minimum-security domestic facility this time. One I was accustomed to. One I shared with my family, a few extra persons and a legion of demons. My eyes landed on the back of my mother's neck. It was as stiff as a forgotten mannequin. I tried to put myself in her shoes but afraid of heights as I was, I found her footwear far too high to tackle.

There was at least one thing I was looking forward to at home. The swimming pool. I couldn't swim so it was clearly not for the obvious reasons. Besides, our pool was almost always desert-dry because of the city council's inefficient water supply, but I preferred it that way. I had long ago developed a habit of going out to our waterless pool with a torch or candle on certain evenings. I would sit comfortably in its emptiness with a book and read until daybreak began to send warning signals of its impending arrival. I didn't know exactly why I had formed this unlikely habit, but one thing I knew was this owlish ritual I practised afforded me a type of euphoric peace otherwise generally lacking in everyday life. Mother always forbade me from staying outside in the yard late by myself. "What if some murderous burglars were to find you? God forbid!" But of course, I paid her no mind. And unfortunately, no homicidal criminals ever discovered me. So that night I was going back to my nightly haunt to once more drown my melancholies and sink my devils until dawn beckoned.

***

"You chased my dad away with your depressing mental asylum tale," Pan's annoyed voice slices through my memories.

"I wasn't aware I was speaking aloud," I mutter moodily.

My eyes search the room for Grandmother's bitter phantom, but it appears she has chosen to make a stealthy exit without my noticing. I sigh with relief.

"So did you go back?" Pan asks, trying to sound uninterested.

"Go back where?" I absently ask in return.

"To visit Benzi. Did you keep your word? But of course, being of the female gender you probably didn't," is his coarse reply.

I throw him a wilting look and say, "Actually I did visit. Or at least I tried to. I went back one week after I was discharged and he was…well, he was gone. They told me he simply vanished the day after I left, most likely ran away. Not a single fragment of him remained. I remember leaving that place feeling rather damp. I try never to wonder what happened to him, so don't bother asking me what my conspiracy theories are on the matter because I don't have any."

A heavy silence descends until Pan dryly notes, "Your tragedy, my dear, is that you fall too effortlessly into the pit of romance. It will be your undoing."

"Don't sound so condescending. Especially since you yourself are already undone by lust," is my retort.

"That is of course a falsehood. But being human, you're entitled to your errors of judgement. Anyway, let's just hope you don't run into poor crazed Benzi roaming the streets of our once sunlit but now darkened city, clutching a plastic bag full of illegible papers, talking to no one in particular about divine typewriters. That's if the fellow ever existed to begin with. Let's not forget you were committed for befriending your own hallucinations," he remarks pointedly.

I do not try to hide my irritation. "Benzi was not a creation of my grossly misunderstood imagination. He was real. I'm sure if you care to visit that institution of horrors I was committed to you'll find him in the records. On what might have happened to him or where he may be, I told you I won't speculate and I meant it. Now can we drop the subject?"

"Subjects are, by their very nature, designed to fall and be picked up again when suitable."

"You bore me sometimes," I tell Pan flatly.

He responds by grimacing rather theatrically. I smile despite myself. He takes this as an opportunity.

"As disillusioned as we're both apparently feeling, we might as well fuck," he declares in his wisest voice.

"That's unlikely to happen anytime in the foreseeable future. My state of mind and my mood won't allow it. But you can dial up Veronique for a second helping if you're that hungry," I say in the sweetest of voices. He scowls.

"Your attempts at sarcasm are always fantastic fails. I find it very ironic that I lost my virginity to a closet lesbian." His eyes scan my features for a reaction.

My face is expressionless as I retort, "You are the most primitive person I know. The most asinine too. On the issue of virginity, you should passionately thank your gracious gods they made you lose your purity to someone of my calibre. If I were you, I'd take it as an undeserved honour."

I hear him growl and for the briefest of moments, he resembles a wild animal. He hisses under his breath and turns away from me. I ignore him intently and observe the minutes struggling by. A thin layer of misogyny settles its fine dust on my skin, nonchalantly. My flesh is in urgent need of a baptism of sorts…or something. I'm stuck. I must have swallowed a bucket of inertia…or nothing. My wheels stubbornly decline to move, my engine is rusted iron. The machinery of self has ground to a sluggish halt. It refuses to cooperate. I remain rooted in my crumbling foundations, waiting for the inevitable collapse. The eventual demise.

We eat our pizzas and come to a general consensus to exit the bizarre walls of Pan's flat. He remembers that today is the deadline for submissions for a lucrative Western-funded exhibition-cum-competition at the main art gallery and decides he wants to submit. And besides, we really have to escape the creeping claustrophobia subtly starting to permeate the air. We waste no time gathering up our dismembered parts and crookedly stitching them back on. They seem to dangle limply off our torsos like a defeated generation. Our generation. I watch Pan throw assorted paraphernalia into his rucksack. I tell him to include his camera among the other particulars he's carrying, at the same time as I cynically wonder what original sights could one possibly still collide with in these sapless times. "Isn't everything old under the clouds?" a whisper resonates and I nod my head. After taking what is required, we leave.

The city meets us with a frantic embrace. It teems with a population resigned to its anguish, a people static in their dejection. They line the cracked pavements, circle the dizzying streets and square off in suffocating slums. They triangulate in segregated zones of cowed submissiveness.

They scratch their fleas in the markets and coagulate in god-zealous congregations that staunchly refuse to visualise the invisibility of their deity. They languish and lament and yet stoically receive the lethal lashes daily dished out to them by a hand rumoured to be infallible. They meekly swallow the faecal matter of their lives and only permit themselves the relief of vomiting out their frustrations in the privacy of their insignificant perimeters. They are the *povo*, the forgotten masses, and they lack the luxury of thinking about insurrections. Or so it is generally believed. But then you take a moment to study their eyes, hard as granite, and you hesitate…

We weave our way through the crowd of repressed desperation. Pan narrowly dodges being rammed to the ground by a pirate taxi blindly fleeing two unhelmeted police officers on a motorcycle. Across the road, a plainclothes municipal policeman is savagely pulling a basket of vegetables from the determined arms of a female vendor. To the side, a young woman with ample hips sashays past, wearing a sculpted miniskirt. She immediately arouses the attention of a pack of restless male wolves who stir and begin to sniff her excitedly. Her oblivious legs are soon to be the centre of an uncontrollable testosterone frenzy and I feel a jab of sympathy. Meanwhile, Pan and I stride on as we sleepwalk through the insomniac town, our dreams leaking onto the asphalt.

"Something vital is missing in this city," I remark thoughtfully.

"This village you mean," Pan corrects me.

I overlook what he has just said. "Effort? Opportunity? Or maybe both?" I ask no one in particular.

"And that surprises you? This place was a stillborn idea from its conception, an abortive attempt. It's your typical third world pseudo-city. A failure from the first. As we speak, we are stepping and walking on a stereotype; you, me and all these other urban peasants you see," he says and I cringe despite myself.

"I don't agree with your pessimism. And the term 'third world' bothers me a lot. It doesn't sit well with me, it's just so damn hierarchical," I let out crossly.

Pan throws me a diagonal look. "Vaginas and random emotional outbursts have been known to go hand in hand," he mumbles.

"Piss off, will you," is my taut response.

We walk the rest of the way to the gallery in a kind of hostile silence. As I put one foot in front of the other, I am aware of a sensation akin to bricks collapsing. Another ephemeral episode in which I silently wrestle against the acuteness of breaking down, of tumbling mercilessly to the ground. I grit my teeth and rummage through the drawers of my teetering brain. What I hope to find is unclear, but its shape is a sort of brilliant normalcy, a glittering mundanity. With great effort, I manage to regain my grip on the weak thread that holds what consists of me together. The entire secret ordeal lasts approximately a minute but still manages to leave my senses bloodied and my defences injured. "Every waking moment is a scourge…" – the first words of a poem I must exorcise when I get the opportunity, I inform the wind. It breezes by indifferently, refusing to acknowledge me.

We reach the art gallery and Pan joins the not so long queue of other unknowns like himself waiting for their work to be assessed and graded. Looking at the hopeful expressions on their youthful faces, I conclude that the artistic life of the average sub-Saharan African is generally a humbling, almost humiliating, experience that requires not only the swallowing, but the complete shitting out, of one's pride. Unable to bear this kind of unclothed hunger – the kind that has nothing to do with famine or malnutrition but a subtler, less coarse, more insidious kind of starving – I tell Pan I will wait for him outside, in the garden at the back. He nods absent-mindedly, his face a quilt of anxiety.

I step out and take a moment debating with myself whether to sit on the grass or on one of the few unoccupied stone benches. As I am trying to decide, I notice two hands energetically waving in my direction from the other end of the garden. I squint myopically and try to establish who the owners of the hands are, but they are too far. I have a habit of not wearing my spectacles in public out of the conviction they make me appear even less attractive than I already am. I resolve to risk minor embarrassment – in the event the waves are meant for someone or some object other than myself – by going over and seeing who it is. As I approach, recognition dawns.

One of the hands belongs to Sheba. My self-esteem nosedives as if on cue. Sheba and I went to the same high school, but that's about the only common denominator between us. You see, she epitomises what I know I will always strain to be. Dazzling, wondrous, diabolically beautiful. She is casually stylish in a vest, palazzo pants, sandals and designer sunglasses. Her rich head of natural hair is tied in a woolly ponytail. Without the assistance of any cosmetic product, she manages to exude an iridescence that stuns and stunts. She recently graduated with a degree in Fine Art. She was initially meant to do Architecture but decided it really wasn't for her. She describes herself as "an unapologetic libertine with no sympathy for morality". At least that's what it says on the 'Bio' section of one of her social media profiles. Her car happens to be a vintage vehicle painted the colour of jacaranda flowers. She is named after a legendary Biblical queen. And it seems she is the all-consuming religion of just about every man who comes in contact with her. Whenever I meet Sheba, I am overrun by a sickening inferiority. Her presence negates mine, it reminds me of all my glaring impossibilities, but I know this is not intentional on her part. She cannot help overshadowing and diminishing those like me, she was simply constructed that way.

The other hand belongs to Shavi. I know him for his almost otherworldly ability to mould fascinating shapes out of a myriad of materials. He is renowned for his grotesquely exquisite sculptures that hint at macabre areas of the subconscious. I envy his seemingly ceaseless bouts of inspiration, since my own creative spring seems to have dried up light years ago. I also know Shavi is haplessly infatuated with Sheba. I doubt the feeling is reciprocal, but she doesn't discourage his affections for reasons best known to her secret intentions. He is an almost permanent fixture wherever Sheba is, enduringly tolerating her outrageous flirtations with other men. He is the epitome of a devotee, one of many, but at least he lays claim to the title 'most steadfast'.

When I reach where they are, Shavi informs me Sheba has recently had a near death experience. I ask what happened, was it a car accident?

"It was a razor and dozens of pills," he says. That's when I notice the bandages around Sheba's wrists.

"Why would perfection want to annihilate itself?" I ask her, confused.

"Because perfection is a painful mirage, an unbearable hoax. Better to eliminate oneself than sustain the agony of a fraudulent existence," is Sheba's reply. "You should try it."

"Try what?" I query.

"Self-annihilation."

"I already have. Poison. They found me before I fell off the edge permanently. I haven't tried again only because of a fear of failing again," I inform her. She nods knowingly.

"I prefer sharp objects. This is my second try. The third will be final," she announces decisively. I smile sadly at the thought of our suicidal sorority.

Shavi ventures an explanation. "Alienation is the root of it. A widening remoteness and detachment that refuses to be bridged. One can't help but fall headlong into the gap," he states. "These are futile times we're living in. I remember the days a handful of us would meet in the park. We were all twenty-something, jobless and godless. We would discuss the ghost of Marechera, post-colonial failed states and the absolute necessity of embracing nihilism as a personal philosophy. The boys romanced European women and the girls secretly loved the boys. We thought of ourselves as dagga-smoking, third world hippies, but in truth we were merely clinically depressed children in denial. With our matted hair and undiagnosed psychosis, we kept on going, never losing sight of the concrete beneath our feet. We were the unsung poems of our time. When one of us surrendered and slit his throat open on a sunny day in full view of our windowless eyes, we knew the implosion had begun."

A pause, then I ask Sheba and Shavi what they are currently working on.

"I'm doing a series of self-portraits that I'm using for personal psychoanalysis. They are quite peculiar. I'll show you when you visit," Sheba says.

Shavi tells me he is blocked for the first time in his creative life. I express my surprise.

"I know what's causing it. It's the fear of growing up. With each day, youth drains out of me and the thought of it is crippling," he explains.

Sheba confronts him. "What's the point of clinging to youth when the electricity has all but gone out of our generation? It's left behind a blank mass of blackness. Sparks like you and I don't stand a chance, our kaleidoscopic nature makes the status quo too nervous. It shifts uneasily in its seat, chews on its raw fingernails, and feverishly wipes its sweaty brow. We have the potential to fascinate, enthral   and intrigue, and no self-respecting status quo would ever allow that to happen. So it pulls the plug on us, leaving us blindly groping for an invisible cause and its unknown effect. We are propelled by a careless anarchy to recklessly argue with curriculums in airless lecture halls because it's apparent the education system is one big conspiracy; to spend our afternoons making love to temporary lovers and our evenings crafting surreal creations; to claim we are serious artists yet willingly break every creative law ever imposed by known superiors. And when we become unemployed, venereal disease-infested vagrants that hang around the city's fringes begging for money, we still laugh in the face of their middle-class superiority and eternally defy their bourgeois respectability. We will never stop painting our subconscious onto the dreary pavements we aimlessly walk or sculpting our psyche onto the public benches we occupy when it's time to daydream, for these inanimate objects will faithfully carry our legacy when nothing else will," she declares.

I feel somehow redundant standing in front of these two unworldly beings, like a newly-dead someone facing her ancestral host for the first time. Pan appears. His expression is a blister about to burst. He seethes as he stands, clutching his submissions too tightly.

"What happened?" I ask, although I already have an idea.

"They said my work doesn't fit the criteria. What fucking criteria? They said it's difficult to categorise, it screams too loud. What in Satan's bloody hell does that mean?!" he bellows.

We all stare at him and a moment of silence ensues. He calms down and notices Sheba. I watch him eyeing her. She is used to this sort of naked male attention and has no problem meeting his eyes brazenly. Something in my gut complains. I don't know if it's dawning hunger or disgust. It could be both. We all take time to properly digest the raw angst lodged in our throats. For a split second, life takes on an indigo hue and the midnight part of ourselves reigns unchallenged. Pan has recovered enough to take out his camera and he proceeds to snap the three of us in varying poses of disillusionment. After a time, Sheba straightens herself and stands up. With the clink-clank of her car keys in our ears she says, "Let's go somewhere. This place is dull. Let's move on, I hate being static," and everyone grunts in agreement.

Pan suggests we go to a shebeen and spend the rest of the day drinking *kachasu*, an illicit brew hot enough to incinerate one's insides. Shavi suggests we visit the colonial-era workers' hostels of the city's oldest township. I suggest we go leap off a tall building. Sheba ignores all of us as she leads the way to her jacaranda-coloured car. As we walk, a mocking wind whips my internal world, and in the process, brings attention to a lopsidedness that can't quite be righted. Pan and Shavi are absorbed in a discussion about the exact nature of identity, and I can't be bothered to join in. I am too preoccupied with my own horrors. When we get to the vehicle, we all pack ourselves into its inviting warmth. As it starts to move Sheba turns on the music. Chiwoniso Maraire sings to us soothingly. I watch the sordid city glide by the window numbly. Sullen buildings, potholed streets, weary beings, shrivelled trees, polluted atmosphere. I absorb it all without a fight.

Shavi enquires where exactly we are going and Sheba answers "Wherever the action is."

"What kind of action exactly?" Shavi probes.

"Explosions and eruptions. At the very least. I'm sure that's what we're all looking for. Am I wrong?" she asks confidently, waiting for the traffic light to turn green.

"And if we don't find them?" I venture to ask.

"Then we might as well smoke some ganja and go home to sleep our miserable lives away," she answers and no one dares say anything more for a while.

We eventually begin to trade our varying migration stories. Sheba speaks of frequenting the opera houses and art museums of Vienna, Pan tells of times spent in Trafalgar Square and along the waters of the Thames, I talk of the canals and the breathing female mannequins in the display windows of Amsterdam, and Shavi reminisces about his days as an idealistic student at Kampala's Makerere University. We drive past a woman sleeping in front of a filthy public toilet surrounded by her rags and baggage and I wonder what her story is. The calm is interrupted by the sound of a text message on Pan's phone. He reads it and a gleeful expression plasters itself on his face.

"I think we've found our action. Just got this text from Lumumba. He says a demonstration is going down right now at the city square and he wants us to join. Are you guys in? I am. There's nothing better to do."

Sheba is already driving the car in the direction of the square, so it seems the decision has been made for us. Lumumba is the pseudonym of an individual who considers himself the country's most radical insurgent. He is an ardent pupil of the works of Bakunin and Kropotkin but vehemently denies he is an anarchist. According to him, his cause is insurgency, period. I'm not sure I actually know what his birth name is or care to know. What I do know is that he has the countenance of a prehistoric beast and lethal inclinations.

By the time we pull up to the scene, we find what was once probably a peaceful demonstration has now evolved into a full-blown riot. It appears the flower sellers who normally line the square have hurriedly abandoned their goods while escaping the maelstrom. The brightness of the orphaned flowers and the vividness of the current events complement each other. We don't wait to find out what exactly we are demonstrating for or against. We automatically propel ourselves out of the car with the force of oncoming asteroids and hurl ourselves into the thick of it. I can feel the weight of my body slamming into objects, humans, air, nothing and everything. Crashing-shattering-breaking-crunching sounds reverberate all around and my nostrils inhale the perfume of teargas. Rocks and bottles are in flight. Tyres flare. One cannot help drinking the sour nectar of thrown petrol bombs. I can make out law enforcement uniforms and riot shields in the midst of the whirlwind. Shouts, screams, hollers, howls, shrieks, screeches, cries assault my inner ear. It's so chaotic my head starts to feel as light as helium, and for a moment I'm convinced I have defied gravity because I swear I'm flying. Whatever impacts and blows I'm receiving are painless – or maybe I'm paralysed from the crown of my head down – and I simply surrender to the commotion happening both around and inside me. I'm sucked into the heart of the fight and buckle down to try and protect what little remains of me.

From the corner of my eye I glimpse Lumumba with his fangs bared, lunging wildly at some unfortunate target. He is bleeding from the mouth and the side of his head, but from the look on his face that is not enough of a deterrent. I have lost sight of my three companions, and all I can manage as I'm being swept along by the mayhem is to hope they are alright somehow. If only I could get my hands on Pan's camera. I visualise the magnificent photographs I could take from this particular scene and mournfully regret that I will be leaving empty-handed. My body is sinking in debris and my eyes are stinging nettles. By now I'm crawling on all fours, trying to navigate through flailing legs and inert bodies. My mind is hazy. I'm moving on autopilot. Hell is nearer than it's ever been, but still I stubbornly refuse to ask for divine help. I'm content with my version of mortality, whether it ends this moment or chooses to senselessly continue. From some place not too far away, I hear a sharp crackling sound and night-time descends. I'm anaesthetised in a lake of darkness and my body slumps.

I come back to consciousness in a dim, cramped space. I'm sprawled out on the cool floor. I touch myself all over to ascertain whether I am all there, to check if there are any missing limbs, teeth or eyes. I seem to be in good shape except for a shallow gash on my forehead. I sigh weakly with relief. My eyes try to adjust to the low light so I can take in my surroundings. I quickly realise I'm not alone when I make out a number of shadowy figures strewn around me. I'm in a jail cell. I have been arrested along with other demonstrators. I call out Pan's name, then Sheba's, and lastly Shavi but there is no response. I shudder. On a whim I call out for Lumumba. From an uncertain region of the cell, a hoarse whisper startles me by saying, "Over here." I crawl to where I think the sound emanated from and manage to locate him. I can sense he is gravely wounded. I position myself by his side.

In words reminiscent of subversion he begins to give voice to defiance, "By confining us they think they have conquered, but theirs is a Pyrrhic victory. They have forgotten the incendiary time when the mothers of the land were fed up, when their wombs gave life to caustic terror and other dreaded weapons. We watched as they returned to the bush to dig up their prodigal umbilical cords with their fingers. After this damning act it was only a matter of hours before their disappointment ignited. And when it did, the children and the fathers could only look on as the republic's newly minted amazons pounded the potholed tarmac with the ferocity of furious feet, as they journeyed to confront Headquarters. As they moved, their sweaty doeks sang protest songs, while their blazing skirts toyi-toyied frenziedly like revolutionary ballet dancers. A voice like a Kalashnikov accompanied them chanting, 'Your state-sanctioned witch hunts stand hapless before these once dormant but now revived spirits of the land whose ether you cannot burn at any stake. Their breath is gasoline and their intent a funeral pyre!' The women's temperature rose unnaturally high as they left coals in their wake. The earth scorched itself as an act of deference to their rekindled dark flames and the degrees rose with each forward footstep. As the kettle reached boiling point, it began to rock and whistle ominously. Headquarters waited coolly with frozen fingers and frosty phalluses. These deranged women could never thaw its glacial demeanour so it ignored the kettle's wail and the ascending steam. Finally, the mothers arrived; they seemed to bring the equatorial sun with them. The air conditioners in Headquarters slowly started melting, and those in big offices stripped off their jackets and loosened their ties as the candle burned deeper. The mothers stood rooted to the exhausted concrete, fuming. They said nothing but their bodies resembled atom bombs. The mouths in Headquarters turned dry and parched as a refreshing breeze caressed the waiting women. Only in that moment did anyone notice the mothers each holding a tin can. What for? 'For fuel!' the Kalashnikov voice yelled and the desert wind watched from a distance. They uniformly splashed themselves with the contents of the cans and proceeded to spit at the foundations propping up Headquarters, with matchboxes in hand. They opened their boxes and promptly lit themselves with the failure of the land. Oh, how they shone bright, their wooden frames engulfed in orange and yellow, our beloved mothers. In that moment we knew the times had exploded. Those of us left behind followed their smoking trail, our limp organs more impotent than ever, picking up the charred remnants of our volcanic goddesses. As hungry and emaciated as we were, we could not eat the fried flesh they had so generously provided us. All we could do was stand and think of Molotov cocktails as we looked at Headquarters, the embers in our eyes quietly glowing."

Soon after uttering his tale Lumumba loses consciousness, but not before he manages to hand me a crumpled envelope. I attempt to revive him, but he is unresponsive. A heatwave seems to blow through the cell and I wipe the sweat beads off my wounded forehead. Blood and water mingle and an image of a man on a cross flashes brightly. I shake my head and blink furiously. I cannot afford to unhinge now. I wonder when I will be released, if ever. At some point, sleep steals me and I watch myself wander across the topography of my dank dreams. I am awoken by a displeased hand lifting me roughly by the elbow. It informs me I have been released. Apparently, some human rights organisation has paid bail for everyone in the cell. The only person not allowed to leave is the still unconscious Lumumba. I try not to imagine what they are going to do to him.

I guiltily lap up the thought of freedom in large thirsty gulps, but before we are let go, the police have some paperwork to complete. I know the amount of bureaucracy that involves, so I get comfortable for a long wait before tasting liberation. I'm in the reception area of the police station where a portrait photo of the nation's leader beams down at me from his vantage point. Something about his unwavering gaze makes me look away quickly. My impatient nature makes the process seem unbearably longer than it actually is but eventually my name is called. A hungry looking policewoman hands me my handbag and cell phone, along with a warned-and-cautioned statement. She robotically instructs me to stay away from trouble, or I will find myself back here for a more permanent stay. I nod obediently and try to keep a scowl from settling on my face. They release me and as soon as I step outside, I realise I have no idea where to go. I feel stranded. My mind feels sedated. I am so off-centre I have to sit down on the pavement to try and knit myself back together. I consider going home, but an image of my mother's lotions, powders and lightening creams neatly arranged on the dresser of my parents' too-spacious bedroom enters my thoughts and I feel like ripping off my skin, layer by layer. Home is certainly out of the question.

I remain seated for an indefinite amount of time and then I remember Lumumba's envelope. Scrawled on its front are the words '*To An Old Friend*'. I open it gingerly and begin to read: "*Do you recall the days you and I drank gallons from the fountain of youth? Back then your cause was your master. Your hair grew long and your mouth spoke bullets. You were beyond fearless; you were the wildest animal in town. A crazy cowboy who rode feral stallions, you were the type that ate risk for dinner. The women adored you, they would melt in your presence, but you never let yourself get infatuated. You had no time for romance or frivolities, you were too engrossed in the business of orchestrating coups and composing uprisings. There was something grand in the way you wore your rebellion, something reminiscent of Bolivar or Sankara. Your mind was a handmade samurai sword celebrated as the sharpest dagger in the land. Publications quoted you and self-styled radicals courted you. Many joked that you were so far left you were virtually off the radar. Your silhouette cut a familiar figure strolling through the slums in your fatigues, saying words that left a hopeful taste in the mouths of onlookers. When they relegated you to solitary detention you cheerfully proclaimed that the prayers of the masses kept you company. When they set fire to electric wires on your testicles, you calmly declared you never intended to be anyone's father in the first place. When they tried to hang you, the hangman resigned and the rope stayed unemployed. Your prison letters became required reading, and the urban youth painted murals of your riotous face in every square and in every corner. You dominated and you still do, only now your influence is of a different kind because now you have mastered the cause. When they could not confine you for much longer, the gates yawned one lazy southern day and you appeared like a mirage in the Kalahari, your combat boots kissing the soil. The waiting crowd surged forward in an attempt to collide with your liberation, and your militant lips parted to reveal teeth the colour of cocaine, as you laughed with the abandon of a newly dumped baby. Your release caused such mass hysteria the system fainted. After this seminal moment it was only a matter of weeks before you ascended the heights. The day of your coronation, the stadium overflowed with promise and potential, and the peasants reverently watched as you approached your throne. Is that you my friend? Is it you resplendent in gold and leopard skin, glittering from the proceeds of well-earned adoration? Is that you, the tiny speck on a massive stage too distant for the multitudes to even brush the hem of your garment? Who is that elaborate woman next to you with skin like a grown-up banana and manufactured hair? They say she smells like flowers and wears your ring, is that true my friend? Is she your Eva Peron, or possibly your Imelda Marcos perhaps? I hear nowadays you bath in oil and digest diamonds for breakfast, tell me if that's fact my friend. Do the people's prayers still reach you across those impossibly tall walls you have elected – sorry for that slip of the tongue – I meant erected for yourself? If I didn't know better, I would say you were hiding, but what should one as desired and admired as you have to fear? Your image is ubiquitous and your subjects – pardon me – I mean your comrades tremble with joy at the mere sight of you. See how they tremble and shiver, how they react so violently to your presence. Look at how the people speak so passionately about you on the televisions and radios, literally felling each other – I mean falling over each other to sing your propaganda – sincerely beg your pardon – I mean your praises. I'm glad power hasn't corrupted you my friend, but I was disappointed by your welcome when I showed up at your villa gates asking for an audience with you. I simply wanted to catch up and reminisce on times and revolutions past with an old friend, but instead boots, fists and chains greeted me. Why so hostile my dearest companion? But anyway, being the irrational optimist that I am, I find myself quite glad you've afforded me the opportunity to pen this, my own prison letter. For such an honour I am eternally indebted to you. Until we meet again, safeguard yourself…"*

I stare at the letter limply before stuffing it in the pocket of my jeans and standing up cluelessly. I let my feet lead me to devil-knows-where; I am far too lost to try and make sense of things. As I walk, I avoid eye contact with those I pass. I don't need them to see the broken glass in my eyes, the mutilated mirror glinting sadly back at them. I walk past a cheap fast-food outlet and notice a familiar face serving customers from behind the counter. The face belongs to a young woman I know. We were at university together, the first university I dropped out of. Unlike me, she completed her Engineering degree, and now she spends her hours selling oily food to strange people. How lovely.

A purple butterfly flits across my path but I feel no desire to catch it. In fact, I barely notice it. A sensation similar to scum settles over my emotions, forcing me to succumb. I'm becoming more fragile by the second and I don't approve. I look around me. My feet have taken me to a deserted alley on the outskirts of the city. The smell of stale urine mingles with an urge to vomit. Cigarette stubs and empty alcohol bottles lie scattered. The alley is littered with both fading and fresh graffiti. Its colours are distinct and its shapes blend with the forgotten surface. I enjoy this open art gallery for a long while. I imagine the steady hands that inflicted this lonely poetry on these walls without the guarantee it would ever be appreciated by anyone except the creator. Yet here I stand touching it delightedly with my eyes, eating it greedily with my vision.

I am transported back to those tempestuous nights when I was invited along on graffiti bombing missions. We would pile into some willing volunteer's car in the quiet hours before dawn. We would cruise the city streets looking for ideal locations to beautify. When we found a building or wall that we all agreed was appropriate, we wasted no time rushing out, hoodies covering heads, spray cans in hand, feet ready to fly. Each person would find their space and start to indelibly mark it in his or her own particular fashion. Shapes, letters, numbers, phrases, pop culture images, nature scenes, faces, statements, animals, tags, all manner of subjects would be engraved with rapidity. The thrill of partaking in this daring ritual of urban fine art was undeniable. As far as we were concerned, we were adorning the city and that meant we had no intention of stopping. One of us would serve as a lookout. At the first sign of approaching night-patrol police, he or she would whistle or clap, and that was our cue to drop what we were doing and scramble back to the car as fast as we could. It was a serious offence to be caught engaging in graffiti because the state associated it with the brash, sometimes abusive, political writings plastered all over the city. To try and explain that what we did was a creative act rather than an anti-government project would not have been understood, so we fled the police with as much youthful energy as we could manage.

But once back in the car, instead of going home we would drive around looking for the next place to bomb.

I remember the coolness of the early morning air and the feel of adrenaline coursing through my body. Those moments were coloured in shades of zest that turned the future into an unnecessary blink in the expanse of time. A sort of serenity settles above me, and I finally allow the tears to cascade like they have been begging to do the whole day. I cry with a depth that soothes my sores, that deadens my nerves. I fold myself into a foetal position and let my mind regress to zero. I tell myself that this is as close to an authentic religious occurrence as I am likely to ever experience so I embrace it with no inhibition. This is before an unpleasantly rational voice in the corner of my mind tells me I cannot stay in this hallowed space much longer, I have an anonymous destination to reach. I uncurl, pick up my useless belongings and leave without farewell. Maybe I will return, maybe I will burn instead. Maybe I will go down in scalding bourgeois flames that can't be doused by any grassroots pretensions.

As I resume walking, I think of my seven-year-old self and wish I could paint her a pretty picture of adulthood and the failures that come with it. My mood is as grey as a July sky. Terrible sights thump in my head in rhythm with my footsteps. Without realising how or why, I find myself entering the parking-lot of the literary café, the one most frequented by the city's 'arty' crowd. A few cars are parked. Small cliques of people laze around in the empty gaps between vehicles. The thick scent of marijuana floats in the air. I walk over to a random group and join them. The members acknowledge me with casual nods. I proceed to melt into the periphery. This particular group is discussing the fundamentals of hip-hop culture and its relation to urban Africa. I don't participate, I only listen. The discussion is interspersed with spontaneous outbursts of rapping and beatboxing from the different group members, which invariably elicit sounds of approval from the others. As I watch them engrossed in their religious ritual, I feel disconnected, out of socket.

Boredom gnaws at my insides. I leave the group. Nobody notices my departure. I go into the café where an unknown jazz band is playing for a multiracial smattering of people. No one is paying the band any attention. I scan the room and notice Pan speaking animatedly to a man thrice his size. I go over and quickly realise all is not well between them. The foul smell of hostility is palpable. From what I gather, Pan and the goliath are locked in an increasingly escalating argument over a fair-haired, pale-skinned, Scandinavian-looking woman seated nearby. Sizing up the situation, I conclude that Pan is suicidal. I won't be surprised if he finishes the day toothless or, worse, with an okapi knife protruding from his neck. I pull him away and ask where Shavi and Sheba are. He tells me they went to Sheba's house with an assortment of characters.

"Maybe I should go there too. I'm restless," I muse.

"If orgies and excessive depravity interest you then Sheba's place is certainly ideal," Pan says absently, his gaze trained on the Scandinavian-looking lady.

"No, that doesn't interest me. Solitude is what I'm after," I mumble to myself.

Pan shrugs impatiently and wastes no time going back to his waiting argument. The acidic taste of loneliness peppers my tongue. Again, I think of going home but what is there in that sunken ship of suburbia but my inescapable monsters? I decide to just start walking and never stop. My shadow will be my companion. The two of us will roam the earthy roads of the globe and imprint our energy where we tread. Maybe somewhere in my travels I will be reunited with Benzi; I think of him so often. I will sing books, paint poems, carve songs, sculpt films, design plays, dance, move, whirl, rotate, orbit, rise, fly, leak, burst! release! exhale! My system is overheating, my nerves are melting, my psyche is screaming. I never knew losing control could feel so pure, so sacrosanct. I surrender to the inferno in my veins and begin to shout again and again, "My name is Mhepo, daughter of the wind! My name is Mhepo, daughter of the wind!" Grandmother materialises and tells me to go to the mountain, something special awaits me there. I obey her and begin to run.

My clothes feel heavy on my dripping skin, so I free myself from their weight. I want to be unencumbered, unhampered. I am not aware of the people I streak past. The only thing that matters in this moment is the electric rush of air in my ears. The music of drums engulfs me. I am swallowed by a rhythmic chanting voice, a voice from time immemorial. They have come for me. I run faster but I cannot outpace my roots, I cannot flee history anymore. My skeleton rattles as my bare feet pummel the ground in a frenzy. Everything is a haze around me. I increase speed. I am ready to collide with my call, to ram full force into the core of it. There remain no more choices because my chasers have finally caught up with me. This is the last run, the final escape attempt. My thoughts grow wings that soar higher than the black clouds drifting above my head. I flap them with such power a whirlwind is born. It transports me in its womb for a distance before unceremoniously dumping me like an unwanted infant. I keep running, walking, flying, moving. Uncontrollable motion. The whispers of my pursuers brush against my feverish skin. Ancient words caress my surface and mingle with the salty water pouring down my body. I stumble and tumble and instantly lift myself up again. A mad urgency informs me there can be no delay. A dark euphoria raises its head inside me. My heart is a thumping instrument. My engine is a fiery vessel. They are approaching rapidly, I can feel their wails licking my heels. They are intent on capturing their prey, but I am not ready to give in just yet. Their cries ring out sharp and shrill. Shadowy silhouettes knock on the corners of my eyes.

A slow-burning panic arrives and settles in my chest. It numbs the warm part of me and paralyses my vital signs. I try to ignore it, but I can't stop listening to its terrorising wisdom. It takes on the shape of a marauding anxiety that will not allow peace any room, any small space. It is the waking nightmares of an incurable insomniac, the last fruitless prayer of a man destined for the guillotine. Its clammy hands reach out and strangle all the logic out of me. I become a whimpering wreck writhing by the wayside, a breathing cadaver subdued by epileptic fits of dread. I keep moving. My armpits are moist, my mouth overflows with foam. Sometimes the sensation gets so intense I have to levitate to keep from shredding my feet. I think of Pan, Sheba, Lumumba, Shavi, Benzi, my parents, my siblings. I think of the times, the moments, the split seconds, the revolving doors of this life, this inscrutable reality. The movements that never cease.

A mysterious voice from within accompanies me. Words emanate from its invisible mouth: "I belong to a generation flushed down the twenty-first century pit latrine. Children of waste, we wallow in the sewage of our rotting dreams. The foul stench of futility is unavoidable, so we surrender to the excrement of our withering days. Modernity has forsaken us, tradition long ago defecated us. We stand stranded at the crossroads unable to move backward or forward. Even though we see our mangled selves reflected in the looking glass, still we cannot locate ourselves. Where did we go? The space where happiness is supposed to be has caved in, trapping all the precious things of life in its rubble. We burrow underground in an attempt to retrieve that which we lost, but we continue to lose. We meander in search of the gifts we were promised but are yet to receive. The only answers we possess are rage, drunkenness, decadence, promiscuity, addiction, hedonism, suicide, medication, lunacy and the necessity of imagination. Only in telling our stories are we momentarily released from the agony of our fate. Only in recreating our haunting hurts on paper, canvas, stone, stage, screen are we temporarily absolved from the stain of our sins. Our highest goal is to make it through the next minute, therefore every new sunrise is cause for celebration. Our gods are the devils that plague us day and night, the hopes that germinate and die unfulfilled. The elders have betrayed our childish faith in them. Consequently, we no longer worship their authority, rather we curse their cults of personality. We are a bitter brood bringing desecration in our cupped palms. Beware…"

My feet are galloping, I am getting closer. I pass the abandoned railway yard I used to frequent and nostalgia rears its head. I would often make solitary travels to the yard to arrange my thoughts whenever they became too scattered. I would bring books to read and pages to write, and spend hours communing with the decaying locomotives as I hunted and gathered my sane self back together. It became a sort of sanctuary for me in times of dissipation. Sometimes I would go with Pan and we would picnic there, talking philosophy and the uselessness of making an effort in this godforsaken life. Poems were composed and reams of moody photographs were captured. Pan had plans to publish a photographic book of pictures from our times at the yard, but in the end most of them simply ended up on social media, receiving dozens of shallow likes and comments from distant virtual admirers. I also enjoyed conversing with the destitute who made the lonely railway yard their home. They had the most captivating stories of how they ended up in their present state. I would sit and listen as they unwound their tragedies. They rarely asked for much; a cigarette, strong brew, a coin here, a dollar there. Life was a deep blue during these periods. I would catch myself rolling the taste of the fringe around in my mouth and savouring it. I could temporarily forget my anguish and lay in the soft green grass of the current moment. There was no need to try and outwit myself, I could just be. A sense of restoration would lather me and I would inhale the fragrance of things benign. These recollections almost tempt me to stop and linger, but what is behind me does not allow for that. I have to stay in motion.

I pass rondavels, mansions, squatter camps, farms, industries, schools, clinics, supermarkets and banks. Only when the mountain looms colossally in front of me do I let myself slow down. I can feel the end encroaching. My body is wracked with exhaustion, my breathing is ragged and raspy. I quickly clamber up the mountain without knowing exactly what I am supposed to find there. It is now dark outside. I pause and stare at the night sky.

The stars seem to be conversing and the crescent moon is eyeing me curiously. I bring my eyes back down to earth and continue walking. I let my instinct guide me. I am following the call of something primal. This urge to move is coming from my deepest part, from my underworld. It is undeniable. I find myself wondering if I am in a trance but I keep going. Suddenly I stop. I am standing by a stream. The stream seems to be talking to itself, lost in its own reflections. Then I hear music. Its sound strikes me like lightning. I feel drawn to it. I start searching for its source, but I find I can only move in circles, a confused whirling dervish. I recognise the music; it's the sound of the *mbira*. But there is no one else around. At least no one living. I listen for a while longer before continuing my ascent. My progress is slow and tortuous. I slip and fall often. The mountain and its jagged rocks are not friendly. The phantoms that were pursuing me earlier are now hovering above, watching. I shut out the thought of them as I move closer to my destination. Fear will not deter or distract me. Halfway to the top, a strong gust of wind rises and blows with such harshness I topple over. Soil particles deposit themselves in my eyes and nose as I wait for the wind to subside. As soon as it dies down, I renew my laborious pace. A fish eagle appears overhead and begins to circle me, occasionally swooping down low. I know this is a sign, but of what exactly I am not sure.

After a while, I stop in front of a large cave and I am convinced I have arrived. The bird flies away to destinations unknown. The entities that were chasing me begin to crowd around the entrance to the cave. They are hoping to frighten me away, but my determination is ironclad. I walk past them with not so much as a flinch, and resolutely ignore their deathly howls and groping fingers.

The interior of the cave is warm and airy. I walk around until I find the purpose of my journey. In a dark corner lies a heap of objects. A clay pot, a reed mat, a multiplicity of beads, a battle axe, animal bones, animal skin, birds' feathers, traditional cloths, an intricately carved staff, and a few other similar implements.

Grandmother shows herself. "These belong to you. You have work to do. It is good you have finally chosen to accept. One cannot flee one's origins and expect to live unscathed. You have been summoned and you must answer the summons. You will be taught what you need to know about the ways of those from beyond, the unseen ones. You will be instructed, and after learning you will go back and convey the messages. You are a conduit for those who chant in whispers, a channel for them to speak and be heard in these times. Some will call you a madwoman, pay them no mind. You have been called; you have no choice but to answer. There are precious things one can learn from one's beginnings. Receive what is handed to you and yours. It may be the cure for your collective ailment, it may relieve your wanderings and wondering."

After these words she disappears. I take one of the cloths from the heap on the ground and wrap up my nudity. A seismic shift has occurred deep within. I take my time touching and observing the different objects in the cave. I feel both humbled and overwhelmed to be in such hallowed space. I do not know how long I will be in the mountain, but I am prepared to stay for as long as necessary.

I am now at the service of something far more profound than I can fathom. I decide to step outside the cave for a little while. The night air welcomes me like an old friend as I breathe it in deeply. I can feel my ruined house of stone rebuilding itself, granite block by granite block, restoring what was lost and stolen. I hear the sound of a lion roaring somewhere nearby, and instead of feeling frightened I feel comforted. I wonder how I will be received when I finally return to human society, to the land of the living. The future is unknown, uncertain. What comforts me are Grandmother's words replaying themselves in my mind, "You have been called, you have no choice but to answer. There are precious things one can learn from one's beginnings." By embracing my genesis, my interior landscape is altered. I cannot wait to share the sacred fruits now in my possession with those I left behind. They may think me insane again, but that is not the case. I am not mad. No. I am chosen.

ABOUT THE AUTHOR

Cynthia Marangwanda is a Zimbabwean prose writer and poet. Her grandfather, J.W. Marangwanda, was one of the earliest published African writers during Zimbabwe's colonial period. This led to Cynthia taking an interest in literature at a young age. She became active in the local spoken-word poetry scene before embarking on writing prose. Her work is influenced by unorthodox, alternative and disruptive thought and ideas. It is mainly concerned with the intersections and conflicts between the traditional and the modern, the local and the global, the spiritual and the material. She is married with a son.

Lightning Source UK Ltd.
Milton Keynes UK
UKHW040329210223
417369UK00010B/24